Grace,

Enjoy the book!

Love,

Daniel, Esther, Ethan, Sophie,

Sarah Grace

ONCE UPON A
LEGEND

TURN THE PAGE,
SHARE THE ADVENTURE

BEN MILLER

ONCE UPON A LEGEND

First published in Great Britain in 2023 by Simon & Schuster UK Ltd

1 3 5 7 9 10 8 6 4 2

Simon & Schuster UK Ltd
1st Floor, 222 Gray's Inn Road
London
WC1X 8HB

www.simonandschuster.co.uk
www.simonandschuster.com.au
www.simonandschuster.co.in

Simon & Schuster Australia, Sydney
Simon & Schuster India, New Delhi

A CIP catalogue record for this book is available from the British Library.

HB ISBN 978-1-3985-1587-1
eBook ISBN 978-1-3985-1588-8
eAudio ISBN 978-1-3985-1589-5
UK Paperback ISBN 978-1-3985-1590-1
Export Paperback ISBN 978-1-3985-2366-1

Printed and bound by CPI Group (UK) Ltd, Croydon, CR0 4YY

MIX
Paper | Supporting
responsible forestry
FSC
www.fsc.org   FSC® C171272

For Aunty Margery

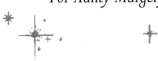

CHAPTER ONE

'Did you hear ANY of what I just said?'

Marcus was in the headmaster's office, again, seated between his mum and dad, a bored expression on his face.

'Well?' said Mr Strickland impatiently, glaring at Marcus through his little round glasses. 'I'm waiting.'

'Marcus,' said his mum, putting a hand on Marcus's arm, 'the headmaster is asking whether there might be a reason you keep misbehaving. Something you'd . . . you'd like to tell us? Something you're upset about, perhaps?'

Marcus scowled. 'I'm *fine*,' he said.

'You see?' said the headmaster, throwing up his hands in exasperation. 'This is the whole problem, right here. The boy must know he's in serious trouble, but look at him! He just sits there, not a care in the world, like he's waiting for a film to start. Demerits, detentions – it's all just water off a duck's back. I'm sorry, but I think we've reached the end of the road.'

'What are you saying?' asked Marcus's mum, sitting bolt upright in her chair.

'I am recommending to the governors that Marcus is suspended.'

'*Suspended?*' she echoed. 'But . . . but . . .'

'Oh come *on*!' said Marcus's dad with a snort.

'Is that really necessary? All he did was move the "shallow end" sign. It was a joke — wasn't it, Marcus? Just a bit of harmless fun.'

'Not for Mr Figgis, it wasn't. He lost two front teeth demonstrating a racing dive.'

Marcus's dad stifled a laugh, and his mum shot him a stern look.

'I'm sorry —' the headmaster frowned, straightening his glasses — 'do you find that amusing?'

'Nope,' replied Marcus's dad innocently, struggling to keep a straight face. 'Nothing funny about that!' He gave his son a little nudge in the ribs and shot him a knowing wink.

'I would remind you,' continued Mr Strickland, reaching for Marcus's file, 'that this is not Marcus's first incident. This term alone, your son has been caught . . .' He opened the front cover, licked his finger and located the appropriate page. 'Putting laxatives in the school custard, shaving the school goat, spray-painting obscene images on the staffroom door, and – let me see, oh yes – substituting potassium for sodium in one of Mrs Brightwell's chemistry demonstrations, thereby causing a SERIOUS explosion.'

As if closing the subject, Mr Strickland shut the file and glared through his thick-framed glasses across the desk once more.

'Trust me,' said Marcus's dad, chuckling, 'when I was at school, I did a lot worse.'

'This is no laughing matter,' snipped Mr Strickland. 'Mrs Brightwell's eyebrows may never grow back.'

'Graham, please,' said Marcus's mum, leaning across the desk and looking pleadingly into the headmaster's eyes. 'Something like this . . . it could really affect Marcus's future. Just give him one more chance.'

But Mr Strickland was unmoved. 'I'm sorry, Mrs Watts,' he replied curtly. 'I've made my decision.'

'Fourteen years I've taught here . . .' began Marcus's mum.

'I don't see that that's releva—'

'Fourteen years!' Marcus's mum said again, louder this time. 'The last three of which, I've been acting Head of History, with twice the work and no extra pay. As well as running the bring-and-buy sale at the school fair *and* the Year Six orienteering course. Marcus isn't a bad kid – you *know* that. He's just going through a rough time. You're sorry, aren't you, Marcus? And you promise you won't do it again, don't you?'

She reached desperately across the table and

grabbed Mr Strickland's hand. 'I know he needs punishing, Graham – but he needs help too. Maybe there's somewhere we can send him over half-term? A week with a tutor, or camp, or . . .'

Mr Strickland looked up suddenly, as if an idea had occurred to him.

Marcus's mum paused, watching him carefully.

'Hmm,' said Mr Strickland.

'Hmm?' she repeated, hopefully.

Removing the handkerchief from his top suit pocket, Mr Strickland gave both lenses of his glasses a long and thoughtful clean. Then, repositioning them back on his nose, he said, 'Well, there is *one* place.'

'Oh thank you, Graham!' said Marcus's mum, pushing back her chair and rushing round the other side of the desk to give the headmaster a hug. 'We'll try anything . . . thank you. You won't regret this, I promise.'

Mr Strickland blushed and shooed her away. 'Now, now, I'm not making any promises. We'll have to call and see if they have room. It's a rather . . . unconventional place. Their methods are . . . unusual, to say the least.'

'What's it called?' asked Marcus's mum.

But Mr Strickland didn't answer. Instead, he reached for the corner of his desk, lifted an old-fashioned telephone from its cradle and dialled.

'Mrs Pettifer, I'd like to place a call, please. To the admissions team . . .' He glanced at Marcus. 'At Merlin's.'

CHAPTER TWO

'*erlin's?*' whispered Marcus's mum with a frown as they waited for the headmaster to get off the phone. 'Don't you think that's a funny name for a school?'

Marcus and his dad shrugged in unison.

'You have?' said Mr Strickland self-importantly. 'That's wonderful news . . . Tomorrow should be fine. I'll confirm. Much obliged. Well then,' he said, carefully replacing the receiver. 'Success.

Merlin's have agreed to take Marcus for the week of half-term, see what magic they can work with him.'

'I don't recognize the name,' said Marcus's mum, a note of anxiety in her voice. 'Is it local?'

The headmaster shook his head. 'Wiltshire. Not far from Stonehenge.'

Marcus's mum chewed her lip. 'But that's miles away! How are we supposed to get him there every morning?'

'You wouldn't have to. It's residential.'

'You mean it's a *boarding school*?' She frowned again, and looked at his dad. 'Do you think a boarding school is a good idea right now?'

'Oh, I think he can handle it – can't you, champ?' said his dad, cuffing Marcus on the shoulder, who grinned.

'There's a lot going on at home at the

moment, Scott,' his mum said, widening her eyes meaningfully. 'What Marcus needs right now is stability. Not to be shipped off to some uptight boarding school in the countryside.'

'Wait, *boarding school*? Would we have to pay?' asked his dad. 'Boarding schools are expensive, aren't they?'

'It's a charity,' said Mr Strickland icily, 'so, no, it's not expensive. It's free. And to answer your question, Abigail, Merlin's is about as far from "uptight" as it's possible to get. The correct term, I believe, is *progressive*. The man who runs it, Mr Tom Sheen, gave a talk last year to the Association of Headteachers. He claims results with even the most . . . *difficult* of cases,' he finished, shooting Marcus a frosty glare.

'Well, if you're sure, Graham?' said Marcus's mum nervously.

'Honestly, I don't hold out much hope. But if you're looking for an alternative to suspension, it's all I can offer. Now, unless there's anything else . . . ?'

And for the first time that week, that term, and perhaps even that year, Mr Strickland smiled.

'What a stiff!' exclaimed Marcus's dad, chucking an arm round Marcus as they stepped out into the musty autumn air. 'I bet he squeaks when he walks.'

Marcus beamed up at his dad, and they both laughed.

'Chip off the old block.' He ruffled Marcus's hair. 'I tell you, the things me and my mates used to get up to at school, you wouldn't believe it! Hasn't held me back. Number four industrial refrigerator salesman in the entire country, barring London and the Greater London area. And I've got the wheels to prove it.'

They had reached the car park, where – as if to prove a point – the sun was glinting on the silver exhaust pipe of a Harley-Davidson motorcycle.

'Old Strickland, what does he know? Has he ever upsold a two-door fridge to a *five*-door? I don't think so,' sneered his dad, extracting his helmet from beneath the cushioned seat. 'Could he maintain customer relationships through the simple power of a pie and a pint? Answer: no. People would be clawing for the exits.'

Marcus's mum narrowed her eyes. 'I've only just managed to prevent him getting suspended, Scott! Can you please not encourage him . . .'

'All I'm saying,' protested his dad, fastening his helmet strap, 'is life is not all about school!'

'But it helps if you get the chance to finish!'

'Sure, sure.' His dad sounded bored now as he swung one leg over the bike. 'Gotta learn to play the system, kid. Make it work for you. And next time –' he winked – 'don't get caught!' He flicked a switch on the handlebar, and the motorbike's engine gave a throaty roar.

'Wait!' Marcus's voice had come out louder than he had meant it to – much louder – and as both parents turned to look at him, the boy felt his face flush red. His dad turned the engine off.

'You're not going?' said Marcus. 'Just, I thought we were going for dinner?'

'Sorry, kid. Got to dash. Work is crazy at the moment. This week I'm in Nuneaton, Milton Keynes . . . Carlisle on Wednesday. Pure madness.'

'Right,' said Marcus, kicking at the ground.

'Now behave at this place, won't you?' His dad

placed a hand on his shoulder. 'I don't want to be back here next week, listening to old Strickland do the same song and dance, eh?'

Marcus nodded and forced a smile.

'Good man,' said his dad, giving him a mock punch on the chin. 'See you, Abi!'

The second his dad pulled away, Marcus's face crumpled, the smile fading as he watched him disappear around the corner.

'You okay, love?' asked his mum quietly as they walked back to the car.

Marcus rearranged his face into a scowl, crossing his arms tightly across his chest, as if he was trying to keep himself from breaking apart. 'I'm fine,' he said, climbing in and slamming the car door behind him.

CHAPTER THREE

'You're lucky the headmaster didn't call the police,' said Marcus's mum as they drove home. 'You won't get another chance like this. Marcus, are you listening to me?'

But Marcus wasn't listening. One of the few benefits of having parents that didn't live together was that you got your own phone, and he'd looked up a photo of Merlin's.

It seemed ordinary enough: a jumble of old-fashioned red brick buildings, linked by lawned areas and paved walkways. But there, right in the middle of it all, was a strange-shaped grassy mound. It was tall and oddly imposing among those ordinary-looking buildings, as if it had landed there by mistake. A gravel path spiralled all the way round and up, and a flagpole sat proudly on its tarmacked top, surrounded by scrawny bushes and strangely shaped trees.

'Is that Merlin's?' asked his mum, glancing over. 'What does it look like?'

Marcus shrugged. 'Pretty average.'

He tapped the screen. In the next photo, a twinkly-eyed, moon-faced man with curly salt-and-pepper hair sprang into view, wearing a strange-looking ceremonial robe.

'Great,' said Marcus, scowling.

His mum stole another glance at the screen as she pulled up on the drive. 'Oh wow.' Her eyes sparkled in amusement. 'Am I seeing that right? Is he dressed as . . . Merlin?'

Something about his mum's reaction suddenly made Marcus's blood boil.

'I can't believe you're doing this to me!' he blurted, getting out of the car and storming off towards the house.

His mum shouted after him. 'Well it's better than being suspended, isn't it?'

Marcus stomped down the hall to the kitchen, where he stood seething at the sink, running water into a glass and watching it spill over and over.

He looked out of the window; then immediately wished he hadn't.

Colin was in the shed at the bottom of the garden, where he always was, tinkering with something or other, usually a part for his stupid old car, Betsy, which broke down every other week. Colin spotted Marcus, and waved at him eagerly. Marcus looked down again, pretending not to have seen him, but his mum's new partner never took no for an answer, and within moments he was heading up the path to the back door.

Marcus turned to leave, but his mum entered from the hallway.

He was trapped.

'How did it go?' asked Colin, wiping his greasy hands on his overalls. He looked anxiously between Marcus and his mum, trying to read the signs.

'We live to fight another day,' said his mum. 'Just.'

Colin's face creased into a big soppy smile. 'Marcus, that's brilliant news!'

Marcus scowled, refusing to meet Colin's eye.

'Marcus is off to a place called Merlin's, over half-term. A progressive school in Somerset.'

'I see,' said Colin. 'Could be worse, I guess. When do you start?'

'Tomorrow,' said his mum. 'I'll drive him there in the morning.'

Colin nodded, taking it all in. 'Well, if you'd like some, er, light relief before you go, Marcus, I'm, um, going down to the air museum later,' he said gently, putting a hand on Marcus's shoulder. 'If you'd like to come, see the planes? Betsy seems to be up and running again, so I could drive us there in about—'

'No thanks,' said Marcus, shrugging Colin's hand away. 'I wouldn't be seen dead in that pram-on-wheels.'

The smile faded on Colin's face.

'Marcus!' shouted his mum. 'You come back here

right now!' But Marcus had already pushed past her down the hall and was heading for the stairs.

'Don't you walk away from me!' she yelled. 'How DARE you be so rude to Colin!'

She ran down the hallway after him. 'You know, me and your dad have been separated for over a year now . . . you need to accept this, Marcus. Marcus!' She shouted up the stairs. 'In fact, I wasn't going to tell you this, but . . .'

Marcus paused on the landing. He spun round.

'Colin has asked me to marry him. And I said yes.'

Time slowed. For a moment, Marcus just stood there at the top of the stairs, staring down at his mum, fuming. Then − without a word − he marched off to his bedroom, slamming the door behind him.

Seething with fury, he snatched up his

rucksack, the one Dad had bought him that time they went camping, and began rummaging through his drawers, pulling out clothes and stuffing them into the bag. He picked

up the framed photo from his bedside table: the one of him and his mum and dad on holiday in Portugal, grinning like idiots, outside that pizza place they had all liked so much. Now the only time the three of them were together was when Marcus was in trouble.

There was a knock on the door.

'Go away!' Marcus shouted.

The door opened anyway, and the tiny face

and bouncing blonde pigtails of Minnie, Colin's daughter, peeped round it.

'Did you get expelled?' she asked, taking a few nervous steps into the room. 'Maybe you can come to my school instead?'

'How many times . . .' began Marcus softly, 'do I have to say . . .'

Minnie took a step back.

'. . . DON'T COME INTO MY ROOM!'

Minnie shrank away from him, backing out of the room and shutting the door behind her.

For the briefest of moments, Marcus felt a twinge of regret. Minnie was only little, after all, and she didn't mean any harm. But then he looked at the smiling faces in the photo again, and something ran cold inside him. Shoving the frame deep into his bag, where nothing could touch it, he made his parents a solemn vow.

I'll kick up such a stink at Merlin's, he thought, smiling bitterly, *that both of you will have to come and get me.*

CHAPTER FOUR

'Look! Stonehenge!'

Marcus's mum pointed out of the car window excitedly. She cast a glance across at Marcus, who ignored her.

They'd left home after lunch, and for the last hour and a half they'd been following a long, straight road as rain misted down from the drab grey sky, and endless boring green fields rolled sluggishly by.

'Can you see it?' pressed his mum.

Reluctantly, Marcus shifted his gaze to the horizon, where a crowd of soggy tourists were staring at a bunch of big stones.

'Yep,' said Marcus.

'Well? What do you think?'

Marcus shrugged.

His mum shot him a look.

Marcus puffed out his cheeks. What was there to say? 'It's nice?' he offered.

'*Nice?*' She twisted to face him. 'Cupcakes are nice. Coloured paper clips are nice. Stonehenge is mysterious. It's magical. It's . . . otherworldly. You know it's more than five thousand years old?'

Marcus didn't answer.

'Some of the stones came from as far away as Wales. But in those days they had no cars or cranes; they hadn't even invented the wheel — so they wouldn't have even had a horse and cart. Can you imagine? One of the great mysteries of that period is how those stones that came from so far away ended up here, in this field, where they still stand today.'

Marcus rolled his eyes, tuning out as his mum prattled on and on.

At least Colin wasn't here to egg her on.

The pair had met when his mum had taken her class to Guildford Air Museum to learn about the Battle of Britain, when the Royal Air Force had fought the Luftwaffe in the skies above Southern England. Colin, who looked after the planes there, had given a talk, telling them all that one of the planes at the museum, a yellow Tiger Moth, had been used to train pilots for that very battle! Marcus's mum had been entranced, and the rest, as they say, is history. Lots and lots of boring, ever-so-detailed history.

'. . . According to legend,' continued his mum, glancing across at Marcus, 'it was built by giants.'

Marcus flicked a mildly interested look in her direction.

'The Giants of Albion . . . That's the old name for Britain,' explained his mum, warming to her theme. 'When the first humans arrived, so the story goes, they had to fight the giants. According to Geoffrey of Monmouth, who wrote one of the very first history books, Arthur and his knights fought the giants in one final, terrible battle. It looked like the giants would win – they were so huge and strong – but King Arthur was clever. Knowing that giants can't swim, he threw their leader, Gogmagog, into the sea. He drowned, and after that, the rest of giants surrendered. Or some say they ran, and hid.'

Marcus scoffed. 'How does a giant hide?'

'Well one story says they disguised themselves as hills and valleys and lakes, then fell asleep. So watch out,' said his mum, chuckling. 'They could wake up any day!'

For a moment Marcus allowed himself to imagine that hidden away in the countryside around them was a band of sleeping giants, seething with anger, waiting to revenge themselves on the humans who had invaded their home. Then the vision vanished, like a popping soap bubble.

He rolled his eyes and turned to the window, muttering, 'Great story, Mum.'

There was a pause, then his mum said in a different voice, 'I'm sorry about yesterday, Marcus. I didn't mean it to come out like that, about me and Colin.'

'It's fine,' said Marcus, deadpan.

'Your dad's . . . he's not a bad man . . .' began his

mum. 'And we both love you, very much. But he and I . . . we didn't make each other happy.'

Marcus thought about the photo in his bag. *Why not?* he wanted to ask. *You used to . . .* But instead he just scowled and stared out of the window.

His mum sighed. 'Shouldn't be too much further,' she said as they rattled off the main highway on to a twisting country lane. 'Oh look! Here we go.'

Two large wrought-iron gates swept open as they approached, and a ribbon of tarmac led them across a windswept field towards a jumble of redbrick buildings. As they rounded the sports hall, the mound loomed into view, like a folded picture springing out from a pop-up book. It had looked strange in the photos, but in real life it seemed even more absurdly out of place, an ancient monument plonked in the middle of an old-fashioned-looking school.

The mound loomed into view

They pulled to a halt, and an enthusiastic curly-haired figure in a blazer and tie appeared out of nowhere.

'Welcome to Merlin's!' he bellowed, throwing open the car door.

Blinking, Marcus nodded in reply.

'Tom Sheen,' enthused the man, his cheeks rosy and a warm smile on his face as he pumped Marcus's hand. 'And you must be Mum, I presume?' He turned to Marcus's mum, his grin widening.

'Hello, Mr Sheen.' She shook his hand, then stared in surprise as Mr Sheen opened the boot, and swung Marcus's duffel bag over his shoulder.

'Well!' said Mr Sheen, shooting Marcus's mum a winning smile. 'Probably best if we say goodbye here.'

Marcus's mum blinked. 'Oh . . . I was hoping I would get to see—'

'Sorry!' said Mr Sheen cheerily. 'No parents allowed! We'll see you in a week.'

'Right,' she said. 'Well if you're sure you've got everything you need, Marcus . . . ?'

But Mr Sheen was already ushering Marcus inside, and with one last confident wave, he closed the door behind them.

CHAPTER FIVE

'So if this is Merlin's, are you supposed to be a wizard or something?' said Marcus.

'Oh no,' replied Mr Sheen with a hearty chuckle, steering him into the depths of the building. 'I'm no wizard, but the work we do here is magic. And it's a very simple trick . . . I'll teach it to you!'

'What is it?' said Marcus suspiciously.

Mr Sheen smiled warmly. 'All in good time,' he

said, striding off down a long corridor. 'We do, however, own a genuine Arthurian relic, if you're interested?'

They entered a library, lined with wall-to-wall leather-bound books. Mr Sheen paused, searching for something on a close-packed bookcase.

'Here we are. *The Prophecies of Merlin*.'

'Wow,' said Marcus, rolling his eyes. 'A book.'

Mr Sheen frowned. 'Oh I see!' he said. 'Very funny.' He gave a light laugh. 'That's not the relic,' he explained. 'Though books, as we all know, *are* gateways to other worlds . . .' Grinning mischievously, the teacher pulled on the book's spine. There was a mechanical clunk, then, to Marcus's surprise, the floor beneath them began to revolve, taking them and the bookcase in front of them with it, before snapping abruptly back into place in a completely different room.

'My office,' declared Mr Sheen proudly.

Remembering himself, Marcus rearranged his look of surprise into one of boredom. Which was hard, as he'd never been in a secret room before. It contained an old-fashioned desk with a dark green leather writing surface, piled high with yet more leather-bound books, a light pink Persian rug and a fireplace with a painting above it.

In the painting, a group of giants were bowing down in front of a man in a red cloak.

'That's Merlin then, I take it?' Marcus scoffed at the figure that looked closer to his age than a legendary wizard.

'Quite so!' said Mr Sheen. 'This is him defeating the Giants of Albion.'

Marcus remembered his mum's story. 'I thought that was King Arthur?'

Mr Sheen looked impressed. 'A history buff, eh?

Well, *some* say they surrendered to King Arthur. Others say that Merlin stepped in and put a spell on them. And do you know what this is?' He led Marcus to a tall, glass cabinet, like the kind you'd find in a museum.

Marcus stared at the item inside. 'A stick?' he said, unimpressed.

'No, no, no, this is no stick. This is far more important and far more valuable. *This*,' said Mr Sheen in a hushed voice, taking a little key out of a drawer in his desk and opening the glass case, 'is a *staff*.'

He took the staff out and showed it to Marcus. Although it still looked much like a stick to Marcus, upon closer inspection, he could see that it was a long, dark piece of wood with intricate carvings along the length of it. The top of the staff swirled together with what appeared to be a dull green stone at its centre. 'This — according to legend – is Merlin's actual staff. The source of all his magic!'

'Right,' said Marcus, rolling his eyes.

There was a short pause, as if Mr Sheen's big reveal hadn't had quite the effect he was hoping for.

'And this,' he said, swirling a gold-and-crimson cloak around his shoulders that had been hanging from a coat stand next to the cabinet, 'well, this I just found in a car boot sale, but it's rather fetching, don't you think?'

Marcus stared at Mr Sheen, a blank expression on his face.

'Anyway –' Mr Sheen sighed, putting them away again, and dropping the key back in his desk – 'just a bit of fun.' He turned back and smiled at Marcus. 'Mr Strickland tells me you like a bit of fun.'

Marcus narrowed his eyes at him.

'How are you feeling?'

'I'm fine.'

'Just fine?' asked Mr Sheen, flashing Marcus a questioning look.

'Yup,' said Marcus, looking back at him defiantly.

'Not worried? Anxious?' Mr Sheen leaned in a little closer. '*Angry*, even?'

'About what?'

'Oh you know, being dragged here, to this educational Camelot you now find yourself in,' he said, gesturing with his arms. 'Merlin's. A week to turn your life around!'

'I won't be here a week,' said Marcus.

'Oh, really?' said Mr Sheen. 'And why, may I ask, is that?'

'You're going to throw me out.'

Mr Sheen laughed and clapped his hands as if he had never heard anything so funny. 'Very good.' He nodded approvingly. 'Very, very good. If I do throw you out,' he said with a smile, 'it will be the first time in the history of this school. You see, Merlin's is different.' As he spoke, he pulled again on the book's spine, returning them to the library.

'We still have lessons, of course, and teachers, and breaks, and school dinners,' continued Mr Sheen, racing off down a corridor so that Marcus had to jog to keep up.

A row of classrooms flashed by: in the first, Marcus glimpsed a teacher being tied to a chair; in the second, rehearsals for some sort of play; in the third, the entire class, teacher and kids together, were just flinging paint at the walls.

'But there's one important difference,' declared Mr Sheen, drawing to a halt outside the final door. 'Some schools only care about what's in here,' he said, tapping his forehead. 'At Merlin's, we are just as interested in what's in here.' He tapped his chest, by his heart, and smiled a mysterious smile.

Marcus was about to give him one of his best eye-rolls when a loud crashing sound came from behind the door.

'Ahh —' Mr Sheen grinned, pushing the door open — 'that must be the Notables.'

The sound that greeted them was almost deafening. In the centre of the room, a tiny girl with curly hair and deep brown skin and a huge boy with kind blue eyes and a smattering of freckles across his nose, both wearing neon-trimmed sunglasses, were caterwauling along to a thumping rock song, surrounded by a rowdy band of schoolkids, who were banging on pots or thrashing at guitars or blowing tunelessly into trumpets, all of them making the most awful, humungous racket.

'Tilly, Rex, everyone, allow me to introduce Marcus,' called Mr Sheen as, instrument by instrument, the music clattered to a halt.

'Ooh, new person! Hello!' said the tiny girl, running excitedly up to Marcus, taking his hand and leading him into the room. 'I'm Tilly. Come and join the band!'

'I'll leave you here, then!' announced Mr Sheen. 'Supper in half an hour; lights out by ten. Rex, if you could show Marcus to his room when you're

41

done musically torturing him! I'll see you all in the morning.'

Marcus snatched his hand back from Tilly.

'What's your favourite song?' she asked as soon as Mr Sheen had gone. 'Tell us, and we can play it.'

'I . . . don't have one,' said Marcus, caught off guard. 'Could someone tell me where the dorm is, please?'

'Yeah, right.' Tilly grinned. 'Can you sing?'

'No,' said Marcus.

'Go on!' urged Tilly, handing Marcus the mic as the band started up again. 'You can just make up the words. It's fun!'

'No, I don't want to!' shouted Marcus above the din, handing it back. 'I just want to go to—'

'Oh go on, have a go!' replied Tilly loudly, refusing to take it back.

'I SAID NO!'

Marcus's voice came out with unexpected force.

Once again, the music clattered to a halt. The first time, it had been more like an out-of-control skid; this time, it was a full-on crash.

Tilly, Rex and the musicians looked at their feet.

There was an awkward silence.

'Are you okay?' asked Rex.

'*I'm fine*,' said Marcus, with emphasis, pushing the mic into Tilly's hand. 'Can SOMEONE just tell me where the dorm is?'

'I'll take you,' said Rex softly. And picking up Marcus's heavy duffel bag as easily if it were a sofa cushion, he led Marcus from the room.

'I can find it myself, you know,' said Marcus, following Rex back down the corridor.

'I don't mind taking you,' said Rex.

'You really don't have to,' said Marcus.

'I know,' said Rex.

At the end of the corridor was a grand staircase.

'The dorms are upstairs,' said Rex as they began climbing.

By the landing at the top of the stairs was a huge window that looked out on to the courtyard. Marcus stopped and stared.

There was that weird mound again, the school flag at its peak waving wildly in the wind.

Rex followed Marcus's gaze. 'Merlin's Mound,' he said. 'It's where the school got its name from.'

'That figures,' said Marcus.

'Though everything in this part of the world is a *Merlin's this* or *King Arthur's that*.'

'Weird shape,' said Marcus.

Rex cocked his head on one side. 'I guess,' he said, walking off again. 'I'm used to it now.'

He pushed through a set of double doors into a corridor, then swung a right.

'Here we go,' said Rex as a tiny dormitory opened out before them, with two sets of bunk beds, some shelves and four small desks. There were clothes and bags and books strewn everywhere.

Though he did his best to hide it, Marcus felt a twinge of excitement – was this what boarding school was like? It looked fun, a bit like a sleepover in a crummy hotel.

'Thanks,' he said, deadpan. 'Which one's mine?'

'This bottom bunk,' said Rex. 'That one belongs to Milo.' He pointed to the bunk above, plastered with chemical hazard stickers. 'And those two belong to Kit and me,' he continued, indicating

45

the two empty bunks opposite, both dripping with football memorabilia. 'We're both Arsenal fans.' Rex grinned, gesturing to the posters above his bed. 'How about you?'

'Look,' said Marcus, 'I know you're trying to be nice, but don't bother. I won't be here long.'

'Why not?'

'I'm leaving soon.'

'Leaving?' Rex frowned. 'But you only just got here.'

'They're going to kick me out.'

Rex chuckled.

Marcus scowled. 'What's so funny?'

'Look, Merlin's doesn't work like other schools,' explained Rex, putting a hand on Marcus's shoulder. 'Mr Sheen *wants* you to express your feelings, even angry ones. He thinks it's good for you. There's nothing you can do to wind him up.'

46

As Rex left him to unpack, Marcus lay back on his bed, hands behind his head. A slow smile spread across his face as he thought to himself, *Challenge accepted.*

CHAPTER SIX

'Morning, Marcus!' said Tilly brightly. 'You've got a good appetite!'

Marcus, who had been working his way along the breakfast buffet, paused. His first instinct was to tell Tilly to get lost, but then he thought, *what's the point? I'll soon be gone anyway.* So instead, he flashed Tilly a fake smile, and continued to add one of everything he came across to the enormous pile of food on his tray.

He glanced up at the clock: 8.43 a.m. If his current plan was successful, he might be home by lunchtime.

The day hadn't started well. He'd deliberately slept in late to try and get in trouble, but no one seemed to be that bothered, least of all Mr Malik, the young, fresh-faced teacher in charge of the dorm.

'Rise and shine, Marcus!' he'd exclaimed cheerily, after ringing the bell for morning call.

Marcus grunted and rolled over.

'Pyjama day, eh?' asked Mr Malik. 'Go with the feeling – that's what I say.'

And that was that: the teacher had left without a word. No argument; no punishment; nothing.

'Seriously though,' Rex had urged. 'Don't miss breakfast.'

'Wait until you try the waffles,' Kit had said. 'They're amazing.'

'And the pancakes with crispy bacon,' added Milo as the three of them had rushed downstairs.

Eventually, however, lying on his own in an empty room listening to the sound of his stomach growling had worn a little thin. After all, he'd already skipped dinner the night before, and he had run out of snacks in his duffel bag. So instead he had hatched a new, much better, plan; one that he was now enthusiastically putting into action.

'Wow,' said Tilly, as Marcus added half a dozen croissants, slotting them between the plates and bowls and glasses. 'Anything else, and you're going to need another tray!'

'I guess I can always come back for more,' said Marcus with a grin.

Tilly smiled and lowered her voice, leaning in towards him. 'The offer's still open, by the way.'

Marcus frowned. 'What?'

'The offer. To sing in the band.'

Marcus blinked.

'The Notables? Let's talk,' she said. 'I'm over there, with Rex.'

'Right,' he said, glancing down at his overloaded tray. 'Great, thanks. There's something I've got to do first, but I'll see you over there.'

Tilly gave him an enthusiastic thumbs-up, then walked off to sit with Rex.

Ladling porridge into a bowl, Marcus put the finishing touches to the mountain of breakfast things he had already collected: bacon, sausage, egg and beans, with a side of black pudding; marmalade toast; pastries; yogurt; fruit salad and a collection of fruit juices. He was ready.

Walking slowly, balancing everything in place, he edged to the middle of the room. All around him, earnest-looking faces were chattering and laughing, eager to begin the day. To his left, Mr Malik was passing the butter to Kit and Milo; and to his right, opposite Rex and Tilly, tucking into his egg-on-toast, was Mr Sheen. It was perfect.

'Good morning, everybody!' bellowed Marcus at the top of his voice.

The room fell silent.

'This,' roared Marcus, fixing Mr Sheen firmly in his sights, 'is what I think of your stupid school!'

And with every ounce of his strength, he flung the entire tray at the wall!

An ear-splitting explosion shook the room as crockery smashed, glasses shattered and items of cutlery somersaulted merrily through the air. For a strange, suspended moment, a collage of scrambled egg, bacon rashers, mushrooms and tinned tomatoes clung to the wall, like a work of art, before sliding slowly down towards the floor.

There was a moment of horrible silence.

Marcus thrust his chin in the air, trying to look more confident than he felt.

The headteacher raised his hands, asking for everyone's attention, and rose slowly to his feet.

'Okay, everyone,' he said quietly. Something flickered in his eyes as he met Marcus's challenging stare. 'Looks like we need to let off some steam this morning. You all know what to do –' he looked around – 'FOOD FIGHT!'

Snatching up a piece of marmalade toast from a nearby plate, he frisbeed it across the room, striking Mr Malik full in the throat!

'Aaargh!' wailed Mr Malik, clutching at his windpipe. 'Right – you're for it!' he said. And, placing a poached egg on the end of his spoon, he fired it straight back at Mr Sheen, who ducked, a yolky mess hitting Rex right in the middle of his chest.

Rex responded gleefully by scooping up a handful of baked beans and flinging them into the air, and soon the entire room was a riot of children and teachers, howling with laughter and mock outrage, hurling handfuls of food at one another.

Retreating back towards the buffet, Marcus watched helplessly as the battle raged all around him.

Not that it lasted long. Within seconds, every croissant had been launched, every glass of fruit juice flung, and every mushroom mobilised. A small figure, covered in scrambled egg, gave Marcus the thumbs-up.

'Nice one, Marcus!' it yelled. It was Tilly.

'Yeah!' called Rex, wiping his eyes free of porridge. 'We haven't had a food fight for ages!'

'Well done, Marcus,' announced Mr Sheen,

flinging one final bread roll in Mr Malik's direction. 'That's done all of us a power of good. Nothing like a little mayhem now and then to make you feel truly alive. Now, who knows who William Shakespeare was?'

'He wrote plays?' offered a girl with ginger hair.

'He did indeed, Carly.' Mr Sheen smiled. 'And poems – some of the finest ever written. "*My tongue will tell the anger of my heart*," one of his characters said. "*Or else my heart, concealing it, will break.*" Now what do we think that means?'

'It means we shouldn't keep things bottled up, sir,' said Carly.

'Precisely!'

'So we should say thank you to Marcus!' exclaimed Tilly.

'Indeed we should,' agreed Mr Sheen. 'Three cheers for our newest recruit! Hip, hip . . .'

'Hooray!' responded the entire room.

'Hip, hip . . .' called Tilly.

'Hooray!'

'Hip, hip!' piped Rex.

'HOORAY!'

Lost for words, Marcus gaped in stunned surprise as, one by one, every child in turn came up and patted him on his back. 'Nice one, Marcus!' 'Yeah, great idea.' 'That was fun!'

Marcus scowled. What was WRONG with these people? Didn't anyone get angry? Why was everyone so touchy-feely? Couldn't anyone say anything to anybody without hugging them, or putting a hand on their shoulder, or patting them on the back? It was so annoying!

'Get off me!' he yelled at the next kid in line, who shrank back in surprise.

There was a short pause.

'You heard Marcus, everyone,' called Mr Sheen brightly. 'I know you're grateful to him, but please respect his personal space! Now, in five minutes it's time we gave our newest recruit one of our famously warm Merlin's welcomes. You all know what to do! Everyone meet on the mound in five. And in the meantime, who wants to help clean up?'

Much to Marcus's surprise, every child in the room immediately thrust their hand up, desperate to be chosen. 'Please, sir!' 'Pick me!' 'Over here, sir!'

'Hmm,' said Mr Sheen, as if he was deciding who should receive a year's supply of sweets. His eyes landed on a pair of children with dark hair and identical features. 'The Tang twins.'

'Not fair!' protested Tilly. 'They cleaned up last time!'

'Fine — assisted by Tilly,' said Mr Sheen with a weary sigh. 'Tilly and the twins, go get the gear. Everyone else, plates and cutlery on the rack, please. Then — to Merlin's Mound!'

CHAPTER SEVEN

'See what I mean?' said Rex with a grin. Marcus was still standing by the buffet, scowling furiously.

'What's wrong with everyone here?' he said through gritted teeth. 'How is that normal behaviour?'

'There's nothing normal about Merlin's.' Rex laughed. 'And trust me, you'll never get thrown out. Plenty of kids have tried; ones a lot naughtier than you. Last year, a girl set the school piano on fire. You know what Mr Sheen did? He roasted marshmallows on it.'

'Wasn't he worried the school would burn down?'

'Oh no, every room in this school is fireproof and waterproof,' explained Rex. 'The walls are built to withstand everything – flames, paint, food. You can throw anything at them!'

'What happened to the girl?'

'She went crazy, of course,' said Rex. 'Shouting and swearing. Then eventually she broke down, started crying. Told Mr Sheen everything. Turns out she lost her parents in a car accident when she was little. The fire was her way of acting out. Soon after that, she stopped misbehaving, made friends . . . She's turned a corner. In fact, she's now one of the lead singers of a very reputable band.'

There was a pause.

'You mean Tilly, don't you?' asked Marcus.

Rex nodded.

'What about you, Rex? How come you're in here?'

'I killed a man,' said Rex matter-of-factly.

Marcus blinked.

Then Rex cracked a smile, and burst out laughing. 'Haha, got you!'

'Boiler suits, everyone!' said Tilly, returning with five bright yellow suits made of a thick, waterproof material.

'You'll want to put that on,' said Rex to Marcus as he, Tilly and the twins climbed into their suits.

'Er, no thanks.'

'Trust me,' said Rex.

'I'm fine,' said Marcus firmly. No way was he messing up his look with that cringey yellow outfit.

'Everyone in position?' shouted Tilly. 'Twins — Hoovers, please!'

One of the Tang twins flicked a switch on the wall. All around the room, the skirting boards creaked upward, like little trapdoors. From behind them came a loud sucking sound.

'Everyone link arms,' shouted Rex. 'The Hoovers are very powerful.'

Marcus gawped in amazement as all the broken crockery and fallen food was sucked across the floor and away into the walls.

'Brace yourselves!' warned Tilly. 'Water!'

'You really should put that suit on,' said Rex.

Marcus rolled his eyes.

'Your call.'

A moment later, Marcus screamed as water rained down from sprinklers in the ceiling. In a second, he was drenched.

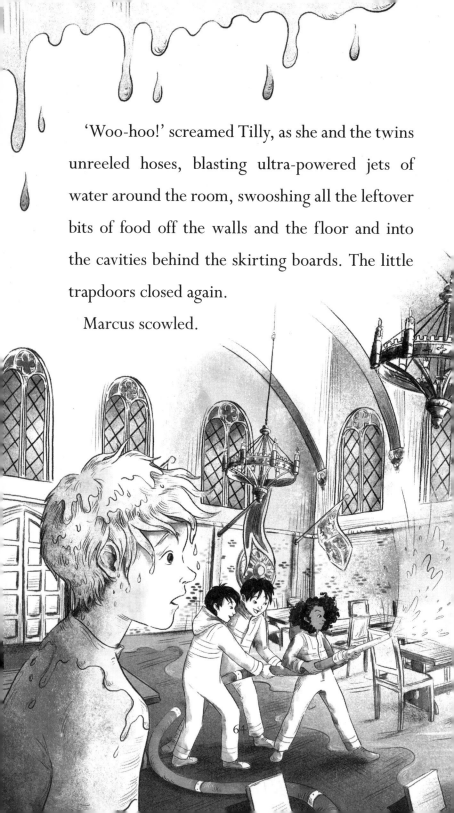

'Woo-hoo!' screamed Tilly, as she and the twins unreeled hoses, blasting ultra-powered jets of water around the room, swooshing all the leftover bits of food off the walls and the floor and into the cavities behind the skirting boards. The little trapdoors closed again.

Marcus scowled.

64

'Told you,' said Rex, grinning. 'Don't worry, you'll dry off in a sec.'

'What?' said Marcus.

'Air!' shouted Tilly.

She flicked a final switch, and a series of vents in the walls began blowing hot air around the dining hall. In seconds, the sopping wet room was dry as a bone, and as clean as a new pin.

And Marcus was too.

'Cool, huh!' said Tilly, rushing over. 'Ooh, look at you, all clean and dry! So now you know – you never need to worry about wrecking anything. Any time you need to let off steam, just go for it. Now quick, everyone, to the mound! The ceremony's starting!'

Marcus followed Tilly and the others in stunned silence out of the dining hall and back down the corridor. He felt like a car that had been through a car wash.

'So,' said Rex, 'why are you in here?'

Marcus shrugged. He tried to act cool and claw back some dignity. 'Oh you know, I did some pranks, caused a bit of trouble, blew some stuff up, whatever.'

'No, I mean *why*?'

'What do you mean, why?'

'Why did you do that stuff? Mr Sheen says we act out for a reason.'

Marcus bristled.

'I wasn't *acting out*,' he snapped. 'And if I was, it's none of your business.'

'You're right,' said Rex, holding up his hands. 'It's none of my business. But it *is* Mr Sheen's.

And trust me: whatever you do, however you misbehave, he'll find out what's behind it.'

Marcus squinted against the light as they pushed through the double doors at the end of the corridor and out into the courtyard – then immediately recoiled in horror.

Standing at the base of the mound, dressed in Merlin's crimson-and-gold cape and holding Merlin's staff in one hand and a megaphone in the other, was Mr Sheen.

Around him, the entire school was gathered, waiting for instruction.

'Greetings, Marcus!' said Mr Sheen through the megaphone. 'Please join me at the front of the procession! Everyone else, please follow behind! Let the ceremony commence!'

CHAPTER EIGHT

Marcus instinctively took a step backwards, but Rex and Tilly were standing right behind him.

'Come on!' whispered Rex. 'It's just a bit of fun! It'll be over in a minute.'

Tilly gave Marcus a gentle push. 'Don't be nervous,' she said, encouraging him forward.

'I'm not nervous,' said Marcus, scowling. 'I'm FINE.'

'You say that a lot,' said Tilly.

'Because it's true,' replied Marcus. And just to prove it, he took a deep breath and marched defiantly over to Mr Sheen, who began to lead the way up the winding path towards the top of the mound. Marcus followed in furious silence. When he glanced back, he was horrified to see that, sure enough, an orderly queue had formed behind him and was snaking its way up from the base of the mound, heading for the flagpole at the top.

Marcus tried desperately to think of what he could do to get himself in trouble. But how did you get in trouble at a school that was built to withstand anything you could throw at it? Where violent emotions were applauded? Angry outbursts not only allowed but actively encouraged?

They had reached the top of the mound. The school flag – a picture of Merlin, cloak billowing, holding up his staff – was flapping in the wind above Marcus's head.

Mr Sheen gestured for the rest of the procession to gather round him and Marcus in a wide circle.

'We are here,' shouted Mr Sheen through his megaphone, 'to welcome Marcus, our newest recruit. Marcus, would you please step forward?'

Scowling ferociously, Marcus took a very small step forward.

'This mound we stand on is named after this country's most famous magician. Legend tells us,' continued Mr Sheen, as the megaphone gave a screech of feedback, 'that Merlin ruled over these lands for many centuries, defeating powerful foes and bringing peace to this great country, using only his staff and the power he held within. It is Merlin that we see emblazoned on our school flag, and at Merlin's we also hope to engage with the forces within us, accepting them, examining them, making peace with them, thereby finding the magic of transformation that lies inside each and every one of us. May yours, Marcus, be awakened now.'

For one crazy moment, Marcus wondered if something magical might actually be about to happen as, reaching forward, staff raised, Mr Sheen tapped Marcus on either shoulder, like a monarch dubbing a knight. There was a glint of light from the stone within the staff's handle – but he realized it was just the sun behind them.

Then Mr Sheen smiled and said, 'Welcome to Merlin's, Marcus.' Before adding, 'All right, everyone, lessons begin in half an hour!'

Marcus stared. 'Is that IT?' he shouted. A hush fell over Merlin's Mound.

'Um, well, yes, that's it, I'm afraid!' said Mr

Sheen good-naturedly. 'That's the ceremony. Bit silly, isn't it?'

'If that's Merlin's real staff, why don't you do some actual magic with it?' scoffed Marcus.

One or two of the younger children giggled.

'Well, that's not the point of the ceremony,' said Mr Sheen calmly. 'The point is not the magic in the staff. The point is the magic in YOU. For you to find your own inner strength and magic, if you will.'

'Pretty stupid, if you ask me,' muttered Marcus.

'You're probably right!' said Mr Sheen. 'It's completely ridiculous! I mean, look at me!' And he held his arms up and laughed a full-bellied laugh that the whole school joined in with.

Marcus felt his blood beginning to boil.

'Anyway, everyone welcome Marcus, then let's head back down for morning lessons.'

As everyone passed Marcus on their way down

the hill, they all patted and slapped him warmly on the back.

'Well done, Marcus!' 'Welcome to Merlin's, Marcus!'

'Don't do that,' warned Marcus.

As hand after hand was laid upon him, Marcus felt something inside him snap, like an elastic band that had been stretched too tight.

He spun round in a rage.

'Get OFF ME!' he screamed, pushing back at the latest back-patter with full force.

A tiny figure yelped, and stumbled backwards.

It was Tilly! Marcus watched in horror as, confusion in her eyes, Tilly caught her heel on the edge of the path, and tumbled head over heels back down the grassy slope, scattering the procession on the path below, before striking her head against a large stone at the foot of the mound.

Everyone gasped.

'It's okay!' called Tilly almost immediately, leaping up. 'I'm not hurt!'

Rex gave Marcus a shocked look before racing down the side of the mound as fast as he could to see if Tilly was all right.

'I'm sorry, I . . .' began Marcus. But he didn't know what to say.

'Her head!' shouted Rex. 'It's bleeding!'

'Stay calm, everyone,' said Mr Sheen as he went to join them, adding to Marcus on his way past, 'Why don't you go inside, Marcus. I'll come and find you.'

The knot in Marcus's stomach was twisting tighter and tighter as he sat on the stairs waiting for Mr

Sheen. He hoped against hope that Tilly wasn't badly hurt. He didn't have anything against her. It was this stupid school, that STUPID ceremony, thought Marcus angrily, his hands bunching into fists.

'She's fine,' said Mr Sheen, entering through the double doors breezily. 'It's just a scratch. She's been looked over by the GP, and she doesn't think there's any damage done at all.'

Marcus felt his body flood with relief.

'I know this was an accident, Marcus . . .' began Mr Sheen. He looked Marcus in the eye. 'It was an accident, wasn't it?'

'Everyone kept slapping and patting me,' said Marcus quietly.

'I understand,' said Mr Sheen, 'and we'll make sure people know not to do that if it's something you don't like. But I just wanted to know . . .'

Ben Miller

He sat down beside Marcus. 'More *generally* –'
he looked him right in the eye – 'is everything
all right?'

Marcus didn't answer.

'Listen,' said Mr Sheen. 'Let's talk, you and me.
You say you're not angry . . . In fact, you go out of
your way to give the impression that you're FINE,
that nothing really affects you . . . But what's really
going on here?'

Marcus shrugged.

'I heard your parents separated not long ago.'

Marcus felt his whole body go tense.

Mr Sheen went on. 'That must be difficult
for you . . . Change is challenging sometimes,
Marcus. It can be scary. And I know your mother
has a new—'

'Why don't you just butt out!' shouted Marcus,
leaping up. Burning with rage, he thundered up

the stairs to the dorm, Mr Sheen's voice ringing out behind him.

'You need to talk about this, Marcus. Or this anger is going to eat you up!'

CHAPTER NINE

W hen he got to his dorm, Marcus slammed the door with a bang and threw himself on the bed. For the longest time he lay there, seething. He hated Merlin's, he hated the stupid kids with their stupid patting, he hated Mr Sheen for not throwing him out and calling his parents and, most of all, he decided, he hated the person who had destroyed his hopes of their getting back together: Colin.

Tour guide at an air museum! he raged internally. What kind of a job was that? What could his mum POSSIBLY see in him? And they weren't even *cool* aeroplanes, like fighter jets. They were the stupid old-fashioned kind, with engines like hairdryers and propellers made of wood. Colin was a dweeb, a plane spotter, a——

There was a knock at the door.

'I thought you might be hungry,' said Rex, sliding into the room.

'I'm not coming down,' said Marcus, turning away from him.

'No, that's what I thought,' said Rex, 'so I brought you up some things. Bit of a weird selection, actually,' he added hesitantly, setting a tray on Marcus's bedside table. 'I wasn't sure if you were vegetarian or anything . . . There's half a pork pie, some pickled beetroot, a bowl of watercress soup, a hard-boiled egg and a packet of smoky bacon crisps.' He paused before the final item. 'Oh, and a throat sweet.' He paused again, his confidence regained. 'If you don't want it, just throw the tray against the wall.'

Marcus couldn't help but smile, and a big part of him wanted to turn round and laugh at Rex's joke and says thanks, but he managed to resist.

'Are you okay?' said Rex. He waited for a minute, to see if Marcus would reply. 'Well, I'll leave you alone then.'

Marcus felt a sharp stab of loneliness as Rex left the room; then his resolve hardened. He had to get out of this stupid place. And he had to do it tonight. He just didn't know how yet.

When he next opened his eyes, it was dark outside, and Milo was drawing the curtains.

'Marcus,' whispered Milo. 'Are you awake?'

Marcus lay in silence, eyes closed, pretending to be asleep. As he lay there, he mulled over his predicament. Sleeping in late, causing havoc at breakfast, very nearly braining one of his fellow pupils: all had zero effect. It was time to move things up a gear. He needed to think of something bigger – something that would make a statement – that would make Mr Sheen burn with rage.

Then it struck him.

What was the one thing Mr Sheen cared about – cared enough about to keep it locked in a glass case – a valuable relic, talisman of his hero, symbol of his school . . . ?

Marcus felt a smile spreading from ear to ear. It was perfect.

'Night, boys,' said Mr Malik, leaning in at the door. 'Sleep well. See you for more fun and games in the morning.'

'Night, sir,' came the chorus.

For the longest time, Marcus lay perfectly still, breathing softly, until he was sure that Rex, Milo and Kit were asleep. Then he ever so carefully raised himself up in bed and swung his legs out from under the duvet.

Sliding his feet into his trainers, and slipping on his jacket and rucksack, he padded out through the door and into the corridor.

He paused for a moment, listening carefully.

Silence.

The cold air mingled with his excitement, making him shiver. Wrapping his dressing gown around him, he tiptoed down the stairwell, along the corridor and into the still darkness of the library. Where was it? Ah yes! *The Prophecies of Merlin* by Geoffrey of Monmouth. Checking no one was watching, he pulled on the spine, just as he had seen Mr Sheen do when he had first arrived.

There was a deafening creak and the bookcase began to rotate, Mr Sheen's unlit study unfolding before him. The mechanism clunked to a halt, and he froze, listening intently. Had anyone heard him?

No. It had worked.

Tiptoeing towards the desk, and using his phone as a torch, he pulled open the top drawer. Exactly as he had expected: there, among the foreign coins and paper clips, attached to a Stonehenge keyring, was a small key.

His hand shaking, he tried the key in the glass cabinet. It fitted the lock perfectly, turning with a satisfying clunk. Marcus opened the glass case and carefully removed the staff.

It was lighter than he'd expected, a shiny, gnarled piece of English oak, polished and smooth. It reached from the ground all the way up to the crown of his head.

The cloak was hanging off the coat stand next to it. Stuffing it into his rucksack, and grabbing the megaphone from the desk, Marcus stole back out of the library and through the double doors at the end of the corridor, into the courtyard.

A wild wind was stirring the branches of the trees. The paving stones were wet from recent rain, and tangles of low cloud drifted across a fullish moon. Marcus sprang up the spiral gravel path, racing round and round until he made it to the top of the mound.

It was more exposed up here, a cold wind blowing in across the inky-black fields, the lights of the main road to London just visible in the distance. His cloak billowing around him, Marcus headed for the flagpole, firmly planted in the platform of glistening tarmac that covered the mound's flattened peak. Positioning himself at its base, in full view of what he believed to be Mr Sheen's bedroom window, Marcus took a deep breath, raised Merlin's staff high in the air and lifted the megaphone to his lips.

'Wake up!' he bellowed.

But the instant the words left his lips, the wind snatched them up, flinging them far away, off into the darkness of the distant fields. He tapped at the megaphone. Was it working? He tried again.

'Wake up!'

He was yelling at the top of his lungs. But it was

useless. No one could hear him. The way the wind was blowing, he could barely hear himself.

Frustrated, he examined the megaphone. Why wouldn't it work? He had imagined lights flickering on all around the school, curtains being pushed back, silhouettes straining to see the cause of the commotion. And Mr Sheen, his eyes widening in surprise, and then narrowing in fury, as the staff splintered against the flagpole.

Marcus gave the megaphone a shake, bashing it against his thigh a few times, then tried for a third time.

'WAKE UP!'

In a surge of fury, Marcus hurled the megaphone to the ground and, grasping the staff with both hands like a golf club, he swung at the base of the flagpole with all his furious might.

There was a strange, fizzing clunk as the head of

the staff broke off, the stone skittering across the wet tarmac. His hands felt hot. It felt good.

Ready to strike again, he cranked the relic back over his shoulder and . . . froze.

From somewhere deep below came a low, rumbling groan.

The ground beneath his feet began to judder and shake and shift . . .

CHAPTER TEN

What was it? An earthquake?

No. The school buildings around him were deathly still.

The tarmac beneath his feet began to crack.

It was the mound.

The mound was moving.

The mound was . . . straightening.

'Help!' bawled Marcus as the flat ground beneath him began to bend itself upward.

Marcus felt panic rising in his throat. He was going to fall . . . He was going to slide all the way to the bottom. He needed to get down, fast. Dropping the broken staff, he spread his arms like a tightrope walker, wobbling towards the spiral path. But every time he took a step, the tarmac beneath his feet was tugged away like a carpet, and he went crashing to the ground.

He crawled back to the flagpole, clinging on in terror, as the mound below him uncurled itself, shaking free of earth and stones, and sat upright, revealing a colossal, ivy-haired, soil-caked human-shaped head at the top of a ginormous back.

Marcus watched in terror as the head turned from side to side, revealing two gargantuan eyes, squinting out from beneath eyelashes of overhanging ferns; two enormous nostrils, exploring the breeze; and a cavernous mouth that

89

opened suddenly in a colossal yawn, revealing two
rows of terrifying boulder-like teeth.

This wasn't a mound at all.

It was a sleeping giant.

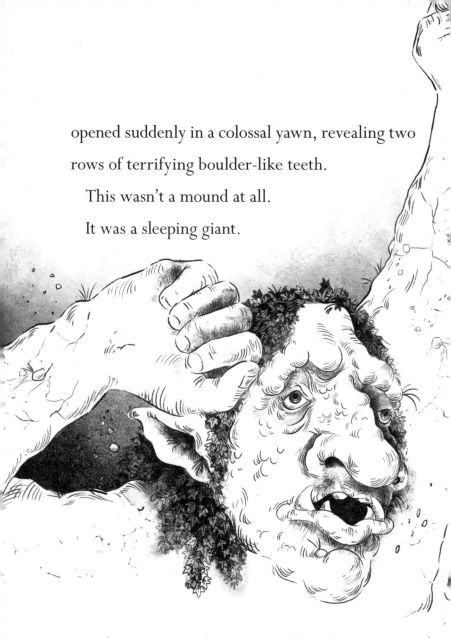

A sleeping giant that was rapidly waking up.

Hugging the flagpole in pure terror, Marcus

stared open-mouthed as the creature rubbed its eyes, seemingly unaware of where it was or what was happening. The low rumbling became a thundering voice:

'Where is Crom? *When* is Crom?'

Was that the monster's name?

The flagpole suddenly began to rise. *Oh no*, thought Marcus, wrapping his arms and legs around it just in time to be hoisted up into the darkness.

The creature pushed itself up from a crouch to a kneel, then began to stand up.

Marcus's breath caught in his throat as the flagpole took off like a witch's broomstick, soaring upward!

'Help!' shrieked Marcus, hanging from the pole over the dark nothingness below.

The giant raised itself to its full height, then stopped. There was a thick silence.

Marcus realized his mistake.

'Who there?' it bellowed, swinging its head round from side to side, trying to locate the source of the noise.

Marcus gripped the flagpole tighter than ever as the monster sniffed the air experimentally.

The giant frowned. The fields and buildings were silent and still. It sniffed again.

'Crom smells something . . . strange.'

With Marcus dangling from the flagpole in the middle of its back, the giant began to spin round and round, like a dog chasing its tail, hunting with its cavernous nose. Just when Marcus felt he couldn't hold on a second longer, the giant stopped and reached an arm behind its back. A hand twice as big as Marcus's entire body came swinging through the air towards him.

Marcus clamped his eyes tight shut, sure that at

any moment the giant's hand would close around him . . .

PEEEAAAARRRRRPPPPP!!!!

A lorry's horn sounded in the distance.

The giant paused and turned its enormous head towards the noise, tilting it in curiosity. Beyond the school, in the darkness of the fields, it saw the bright headlights and red taillights of cars and lorries whizzing back and forth beneath twinkling streetlamps.

'Shiny,' said the giant, captivated by the sight.

Huh, thought Marcus. *It's probably never seen a road before.*

The giant took off towards the lights, stepping purposefully over the sports hall and planting its right foot in the playground. With its left foot, it cleared the reception building and landed in the playing fields. A few short strides later, and it was swishing through the tops of the elm trees that lined the school grounds, as easily as a child might step through a row of daffodils.

But as its trailing foot met the road outside the school grounds, the giant flinched, howling in pain.

'AARGH!' thundered the giant, hopping around on one leg, searching for the sole of its foot. 'AARGH!'

Marcus saw the ground drop away, then rush back up to meet him with each resounding hop!

'AAAAHHH!' The giant sighed in relief as it pulled something off its heel and raised it up into the light.

It was a squashed car. Thankfully, empty.

Holding the car to its nose, the monster gave it a colossal sniff, examining it as carefully as if it had been an alien spaceship. Then, with a dismissive shrug, it tossed the car aside, and set off across the dark fields, towards the whizzing lights of the distant road.

But with its next step came a new obstacle.

'ARRRRRRGH!' screamed the giant again as it walked straight into a bunch of power lines, the enormous pylons that carried them standing silently in the darkness. The fizzing electricity cables sliced into the giant's chest, stopping it in its tracks.

The giant had no idea what these strange ropes were, or what they were doing in the middle of the British countryside. It reacted in alarm, as if it had stumbled into the web of a venomous spider.

'GET OFF!' it thundered, flailing with its arms and legs, getting more and more tangled. 'GET OFF!'

Poor Marcus was thrown this way and that,

the flagpole bucking and lurching like a bull at a rodeo. The two nearest pylons exploded in a shower of sparks, and a thick rubber-coated cable came snaking through the air, narrowly missing Marcus, and filling his nostrils with bitter-smelling smoke.

'WHAT IS THIS?!' screamed the creature in terror and frustration, grasping at the wires with its two vast hands and pulling as hard as it could. With an eruption of sparks, the nearest pylon uprooted itself, sending the giant staggering backwards.

Exhausted, and with the twisted metal frame of the pylon somehow tangled around its arm, the giant began to fall.

'ARRRRRRGH!!' it bellowed.

'ARRRRRRGH!!' screamed Marcus, hurtling with the giant towards the earth.

Though they'd both started screaming at the

same time, Marcus had the distinct feeling that his had gone on for longer.

There was a dreadful silence.

Had the monster heard? Marcus held his breath, his entire body flooding with fear.

The giant drew in a great noseful of air through its tunnel-like nostrils.

'HUMAN!' it roared. 'CROM CAN SMELL HUMAN!'

Suddenly, a colossal finger and thumb plucked Marcus from the safety of the flagpole, hauling him upwards into the cold night air!

CHAPTER ELEVEN

Marcus closed his eyes tight, his heart thumping. *This is a dream*, he thought to himself. *It has to be.*

Cautiously, he opened his eyes to see a vast, unblinking eye – an eye as big as a patio window – staring right back at him.

Then – much to Marcus's surprise – the colossal features of the giant reared back, its mouth curving in alarm and releasing a monstrous, wailing scream!

'NO, NO, PLEASE! PLEASE DON'T HURT CROM! PLEASE DON'T PUT A SPELL ON CROM . . .'

Suddenly, Marcus was falling again.

Time seemed to fold into itself, as what must have been split seconds expanded into minutes . . .

Any moment now, I'm going to wake up, thought Marcus as he flailed and kicked his way through the air. *I'm going to wake up, in bed. That's how dreams like this work. You fall, then just when you're about to hit the ground, you wake up.*

Which was when he landed, hard, and everything went dark.

A moment later, he came to. Badly winded, he heaved air back into his lungs.

His whole body seemed to be shaking.

He was lying face down, his cheek pressed against the earth.

Where was he?

A dim memory flickered in his brain: something about a giant.

Marcus rolled over on to his back to see a vast dark shape looming above him, framed by stars. Sure enough, there it was again, holding up its oversize hands to shield its unimaginably large face, as if from some terrible danger.

'Spare me, please,' boomed a voice like thunder, the saplings that formed the creature's bushy beard quivering between its juddering fingers. 'Spare poor Crom.'

And that's when Marcus realized – it wasn't him that was shaking. It was the giant.

But why? Then it dawned on him: he was still

wearing Merlin's cloak!

What had the monster said, again? *'Don't put a spell on Crom!'*

Marcus's brain at last began to compute what was going on. His mouth fell open in disbelief.

He thinks I'm a wizard! He thinks I'm Merlin . . . And HE is scared of ME!

Was this his chance to escape? He looked up at the giant, its entire body shaking with undiluted fear, the mangled pylon still crackling and sparking on its arm. Marcus almost felt sorry for it. But he needed to play his advantage.

Clearing his throat, Marcus called out in the deepest voice he could muster:

'Yes, I am Merlin! So you, um, better not eat me!'

The giant shook its head, a grateful expression on its face. 'No, no, Crom won't eat Merlin.'

'Or I will put a spell on you!' hollered Marcus, sounding much braver than he felt.

The giant shook its head even more vigorously, clasping its colossal hands together and holding them close to its heart. 'No, no, no more spells, please. Crom is sorry . . .'

'Good,' yelled Marcus, half wondering if it really could be as easy as this to get away from a giant taller than a ten-storey building. 'I am going now.'

The giant's mouth curved into a grateful smile. 'Okay, bye, sorry . . .'

And before the giant could work out its mistake, Marcus scrambled to his feet and marched away, as fast as he dared, through the dark, wet grass, back towards Merlin's.

He had almost reached the stile when he heard the sob.

Marcus stopped.

There it was again. A heartfelt, gut-wrenching sob.

Marcus turned.

The giant was crying.

For a while, Marcus stood watching. Something about seeing this huge creature, slouched on the ground, its arm stuck in a crumpled electricity pylon, its body shaking, its head in its hands, brought an unexpected lump to his throat. It looked so alone.

This is ridiculous, he told himself, and started to walk away again.

But then a voice in his head – a calm, quiet voice that he hadn't heard in a while – said, *You can't just leave him like that . . .*

Hardly able to believe what he was doing, Marcus found himself slowly creeping back towards the giant. Traipsing through the wet grass, until he was standing directly in front of the creature's ankles, he took a deep breath, and said:

'If I tell you I'm not really a wizard, will you eat me?'

The giant stopped sobbing, and a gap opened between the fingers of one of its hands – a dark, bleary eye peering down at Marcus.

'See? It's just an outfit . . .'

Slipping his arms out of the trailing crimson silk sleeves, Marcus held the cloak up for the giant to inspect, before stuffing it into his rucksack, out of sight.

'I'm not a wizard. I'm just a boy . . .'

The giant lowered its hands from its face, eyeing him uncertainly. It wiped its snotty nose on the back of its hand.

Very slowly, Marcus scaled the giant's foot, crawling all the way back up its shin, before perching on its knee, rucksack in one hand.

Looking up into the giant's eyes, he said, 'Are you okay?'

CHAPTER TWELVE

The giant shook its colossal head.

'What's wrong?' asked Marcus.

'Wizard put a spell on Crom. Crom has been asleep, for a long, long time. Now everything is different. Junk everywhere . . .' As he spoke, the giant rattled the pylon on his arm, setting off another avalanche of sparks. 'No trees. Sharp things hurt Crom's feet. Crom —' the giant's bottom lip trembled — 'Crom does not understand any of this.'

Enormous tears welled in the giant's eyes, and once again he buried his face in his hands.

'Crom wants everything back like it was before.'

Marcus felt a pang of sympathy. 'Yeah,' he said with a sigh. 'I know what you mean.'

The giant lowered his hands, and looked at Marcus.

'Boy is sad too? Because there are no trees?'

'No. I mean, yes, it's sad about the trees. But I was thinking about something else.'

'What?' asked the giant.

'Long story. But trust me, I KNOW how you feel.'

For the first time, Crom smiled, and Marcus felt something shift inside him, as if the knot in his stomach was ever so slightly unwinding.

'Want me to explain it all, Crom?'

The giant looked confused.

'You know, the modern world – lights, cars, that sort of thing.'

The giant took a long, final sniff, wiped its eyes, and nodded. 'Yes, please. Crom would like that very much.'

'I need to be back before everyone wakes up, though, or I'll be in big trouble. Deal?'

Marcus stretched out his hand. Crom grinned, reaching down with his gigantic forefinger, gently touching Marcus's palm.

'Deal,' repeated the giant.

'Cool,' said Marcus. 'First, we need to get that pylon off you.'

'Pylon?' repeated Crom.

'The thing on your arm,' explained Marcus.

Crom's expression darkened, the twisted metal clanking noisily and showering sparks as he tried to shake his arm free. 'Human junk,' he muttered bitterly.

'It's not junk,' said Marcus. 'I mean, that one is, now you've squashed it. But pylons are for carrying electricity.'

Crom frowned. 'What is electricity?'

Oh boy, thought Marcus. *This could take a while.* 'Well,' he began, selecting his words carefully. 'So, it's invisible. But it's powerful. And it makes light.'

As if to demonstrate, the pylon spat out a series of glowing embers.

'Light,' echoed Crom. Moving his right arm, he gave the pylon an experimental shake, another deluge of sparks crackling down, illuminating the darkness.

'You see!'

'Light.' Crom nodded, shaking the pylon once again. More sparks rained down, followed by a bright flash, accompanied by a loud bang and a giant puff of smoke.

'Maybe don't shake it too much,' cautioned Marcus. 'Electricity can be dangerous.'

But the giant wasn't listening. Instead, it made circuits with its upper arm, like a child waving a sparkler, laughing as it made pretty patterns in the night air.

'Stop!' shouted Marcus.

The giant stared at him in surprise.

'Please,' added Marcus loudly. 'It could really hurt you. And me.'

Marcus swallowed hard. Had he just yelled at a giant? It seemed to have worked.

'We need to get you out of there,' Marcus continued. 'Hold it like this, then bend your arm . . . then turn it this way, then straighten it . . .'

Marcus demonstrated, Crom doing his best to copy him, the pylon scraping down his arm, sparking like crazy, sticking at his wrist.

'Keep pushing,' encouraged Marcus.

With one final effort, the giant was free, the heap of twisted metal landing with a clang on the ground, still sparking and flashing.

'You see?' called Marcus triumphantly.

'Boy is clever,' said Crom, flexing his now-free arm and smiling. 'Boy is Crom's friend.'

Marcus felt a bubble of happiness rise inside him, bursting into a completely unexpected smile.

'Okay, lower your hand and lift me up.'

Crom, who was still sitting cross-legged with Marcus perched on his right knee, now lowered his immense hand to just the right height for Marcus to step across on to it. A moment later the boy was soaring up into the night sky, butterflies tickling in his stomach, until once again he was face to face with the giant.

'Crom will help boy one day too,' the giant boomed.

'Don't worry about it,' replied Marcus, grinning.

'Crom does not worry,' said the giant, frowning. 'Should he?'

Marcus laughed. 'It's an expression. I'm just saying: you don't owe me anything. Especially as I'm the one who got you into this mess.'

'Okay,' said Crom. 'Now we go see the lights?' He pointed at the road.

'Sure,' said Marcus. 'That's a road. And the lights are powered by the electricity I was talking about.'

'Lights,' said Crom, nodding. 'Not stars,' he added proudly, impressed with his own knowledge. 'Too low.'

'Right,' said Marcus. 'So we just need to—'

Before Marcus could finish, the giant's fingers closed around him like a cage, transporting him rapidly through the air as Crom pushed himself to his feet. After what felt like a few short strides, the hand opened to reveal a dazzling light.

'Ow!' bawled Marcus. 'Too bright!'

'See?' said Crom. 'Light. Made from electricity.'

To his horror, Marcus saw that he was perched high above the main road, right next to a blinding streetlamp!

'No, no,' squeaked Marcus, shielding his eyes. 'We shouldn't be on here. We have to get off! There might be cars coming!'

But it was too late: a pair of headlights was racing towards them!

CHAPTER THIRTEEN

'Move!' howled Marcus, convinced he was about to be involved in a dreadful accident. 'Now!'

But Crom just stared at the approaching car in wonder. 'So fast!' he exclaimed eagerly, spellbound by the headlights. 'And so shiny!'

'We have to get off the road! Now, CROM – NOW!'

At the last possible moment, Crom came to his

senses, stepping off the road into the darkness. The car roared past and, peering out from between Crom's fingers, Marcus glimpsed its driver – a young man, laughing and chatting on the phone, completely unaware how close he had come to colliding with a foot the size of a bungalow.

'Eurgh!' said Crom, pulling a face as the exhaust fumes reached his ultra-sensitive nostrils. 'Smells so bad. Fast, though. Much faster than a giant. Giants are big but very slow.'

'It's called a car,' explained Marcus.

A light went on in Crom's eyes. 'Like the little scratchy thing Crom stepped on?'

'Yes,' said Marcus, nodding enthusiastically. 'They're for humans to get quickly from one place to another . . .'

But Crom wasn't listening; he'd spotted something else.

'Look! More lights!'

Sure enough, on a high embankment, beyond the road, a goods train was crossing through open countryside, led by a cone of bright light.

'That's called a train,' explained Marcus. 'Again, it gets you from one place to another.'

'Hmm,' said Crom thoughtfully. 'Humans move about a lot.' He frowned, his mood seeming to darken. 'That why they get rid of trees? All this used to be trees.'

'Um, I guess,' said Marcus uneasily.

'Hmm,' said Crom. He stopped. Sniffed the air deeply, then, putting Marcus on his shoulder, walked on again. 'Giants like trees,' he said in a low, angry voice.

Trying to change the subject, Marcus said, 'Hey, I bet you haven't seen one of these . . .'

Reaching in his pocket, he pulled out his phone.

He pressed a button, and it lit up.

Crom flicked it a disinterested look. 'More lights.' He was striding purposefully now along the roadside.

'Yes, but it plays music too,' said Marcus, maxing the volume and offering it up so that Crom could hear. 'Listen . . .'

A tinny sound with an insistent beat could just about be heard above the sound of the wind. Crom stopped and smiled uncertainly as he listened.

'What do you think?' asked Marcus, nodding his head in time to the music. 'Pretty good, eh?'

As the song began to build, with a little frown of concentration, Crom slowed to a halt and began to nod and tap his foot in time.

'That's it! You can dance if you want,' said Marcus encouragingly, shuffling his feet. 'Like this.'

The giant frowned, peering closer at the tiny boy wiggling on the palm of his hand. Then he began to copy the boy's movements, wiggling and twisting his hips. Marcus laughed and laughed as a colossal smile spread slowly across the giant's enormous face.

And then the song finished, and there was silence.

Marcus saw Crom's expression cloud once more.

'Good, eh?' prompted Marcus.

Crom walked on again.

'It's called a phone,' said Marcus brightly. 'The sound is called music.'

'Not as good as trees,' said the giant darkly.

'You can use them to make calls too!' shouted Marcus, desperate to keep the mood light. 'And, um, they have a calculator, and . . .'

But Crom just kept on walking, his jaw set.

'Crom wants to find the court now.' He sniffed the air, then veered away from the road again, stalking the plain. 'It is close.'

'Um,' said Marcus. 'Court?'

'Court of the Giant King,' Crom said. 'Big stones. Built by giants.'

The hairs on the back of Marcus's neck stood on end. 'You mean, Stonehenge?'

'Stones, yes. There!' said Crom.

And sure enough, rising into view, dark against the pale skyline, was a crowd of stones, huddled together. Quickening his pace, Crom strode towards them.

Marcus felt a shiver as they approached the circle. The stones were vast, though they barely came up to Crom's knees. Some stood alone; others lay like fallen soldiers.

Crom reached out a hand, running his immense

palm along the top of one of the outer arches, as if greeting an old friend.

'Court of the Giant King,' he said. 'And that –' he pointed to the tallest of the three high central arches – 'Giant King's throne.'

Marcus tried to remember what his mum had told him. 'Gogmagog?'

'Once, yes,' said Crom sadly. Then he frowned. 'Now Tull.'

As he said the name, he seemed to scent something on the breeze. He sniffed again and looked to the horizon, fear flickering in his eyes.

'What is it?' asked Marcus with a sense of foreboding. 'What can you smell?'

'Boy better hide,' said Crom. 'Others here now.'

Marcus's heart stopped.

'Err-umm,' he said, his voice cracking. 'Others?'

Marcus raised his eyes to where Crom was looking. Trailing along the skyline, and striding towards them, was a row of giants.

CHAPTER FOURTEEN

'W-w-what are they doing here?' Marcus stammered.

'Spell is broken. Giants wake up. Meet at Court of the Giant King.'

'Maybe we should leave?' Marcus offered. 'I'm not sure—'

But Crom cut him off. 'Best to hide now. Giants don't like wizards.'

'I'm not a wizard!' protested Marcus.

Striding towards them was a row of giants

'I told you, I'm just a boy . . .'

'Giants don't like boys either.'

'But—'

'Shh, Crom thinking . . . Where is best place?'

'Quick!' said Marcus, flicking a nervous look at the approaching giants. 'They're coming!'

'Nostril?' said Crom to himself. 'No, too smelly. Mouth?'

'No!' bawled Marcus, terrified.

The ground was beginning to shake; the giants were only strides away.

'Ear!' said Crom. 'Come.'

With a deft movement, the giant parted his matted hair, plonked Marcus behind his ear, then covered him up again.

Just in time.

'Crom!' bellowed a deep, rasping voice.

Peering out from strands of ivy, Marcus's

blood ran cold.

There must have been twenty of them, or more — all as big or bigger than Crom.

In the centre of them was a particularly fearsome-looking giant, two heads taller and broader than all the others. He was a truly terrifying sight: straight-backed, muscular, with an expression of snarling hatred on his face. Marcus guessed this must be the king, Tull.

'Crom!' Tull bellowed, stepping over the low outer benches and entering the stone circle. 'The slowest and stupidest giant in all of Albion is here first.'

There was a peal of laughter from the other giants.

'Sit,' commanded Tull.

The gaggle of giants separated, each taking a seat on the stone circle. Like Crom, they were made of earth and rocks, roots and vines. Their jaws were set; their knotted muscles flexed. If they had looked scary from a distance, up close, and all together, they looked absolutely terrifying.

Crom moved to sit down also, but Tull held up a hand to stop him.

'Not you,' he said with a cruel look in his eye.

There was a tense silence as every giant's gaze fell on Crom.

Crom studied the ground beneath his feet.

'Tull is surprised you show your face,' said Tull menacingly, taking up his seat on the throne. 'It was Crom's trust of Merlin got us into this mess.'

One or two of the giants murmured in agreement.

'The wizard betrayed us!' bellowed Tull, thumping the stone beneath him so hard the ground shook. 'I said giants should NOT trust wizard, but YOU . . .' He directed an accusing finger at Crom.

The giants muttered darkly.

'Crom said giants should make peace,' said Crom quietly.

'Why would giants make peace when giants had WON?' bellowed Tull.

Marcus blinked. So the Giants of Albion WON? What his mum wouldn't give to hear this . . .

'Giants should have finished off humans, finished off wizard, while they had the chance,' sneered Tull. 'Then wizard wouldn't have tricked us, enchanted us while we slept!'

More growls and groans.

'Giants have been asleep for too long. Disgusting humans have destroyed our world!'

The Giant King gave a sweep of his arm, taking

in the whole landscape.

The rest of the giants murmured in agreement.

'Trees: gone. Flowers, butterflies, songbirds: gone. Beavers, bears, wolves: gone. Albion now a wasteland, crawling with maggoty humans, every corner filled with useless human junk . . . noisy whizzing things and glary flashing lights. Giants must DEFEAT HUMANS. Giants must TAKE BACK THE LAND!'

'TAKE IT BACK! TAKE IT BACK!' chanted the giants.

Marcus's eyes widened in disbelief. He couldn't believe what he was seeing.

Tull smiled, enjoying the moment.

'Giant King,' he said, doing a lap of the circle, 'must KILL HUMAN KING!'

Madness descended. 'KILL THE KING! KILL THE KING!' the giants chanted. They were shouting and jumping, beating their chests and cheering loudly in each other's faces.

'Where is this human king?' roared a club-wielding giant.

A hush fell. There was a lot of shrugging.

'No idea,' said a voice in the crowd.

'Well how can we kill him then?' said another.

'Easy!' crowed the Giant King. 'Giants will find a human and make it tell us. Then giants will eat it!' All the giants laughed. 'We will find the human king,' continued Tull, spelling it out, 'and make the king, and all king's people, pay for the mess they've made of our beautiful world.'

An even louder cheer went up from the giants. As it died down, Crom's quiet voice could just be heard saying, 'I quite like the lights.'

There was a long pause, each and every giant turning towards him.

No, no, no, thought Marcus. *Crom, what have you done . . . ?*

Tull pushed himself up from his throne, stepping forward until he was right in Crom's face.

'What did you say?'

'Um, nothing,' said Crom, looking at the ground. 'Just . . . the lights are . . . pretty. Like stars.'

'PRETTY??' shouted Tull, directly into Crom's ear, almost deafening Marcus.

Tull pulled back abruptly. He sniffed the air, his face contorting in an expression of disgust as a strange whiff tickled at his nostrils.

'URGGGH!' shouted Tull. He leaned in again and sniffed. 'What is that horrible . . . ?'

Before Marcus could scramble away, for the second time that night, a colossal finger and thumb

came in search of him, pinching the back of his a
jacket, and hoisting him high into the air.

'Well, well, well,' said Tull with relish.

CHAPTER FIFTEEN

Dangling from the Giant King's fingers, Marcus recoiled in fear as a sea of giants surged around him, eyes wide, noses sniffing, faces twisting in expressions of excitement, repulsion and wonder.

'A human!' exclaimed one, prodding him with her immense finger.

'That stench!' said another with a grimace. 'Makes your eyes water.'

'Feel sick,' gulped a third, turning rapidly away and gagging as if he was about to throw up.

'Back everyone – back!' called Tull.

There was a tense silence as, one by one, the giants reluctantly withdrew to their seats.

Tull waited for them to settle, then placed Marcus on the seat of his throne, like a specimen in a laboratory.

'Explain,' he said to Crom menacingly.

'B-Boy h-helped Crom. Crom got arm stuck, in a piece of human junk, and Boy set Crom free,' stammered Crom.

'TRAITOR!' bellowed the king, leaping forward and twisting Crom's ear so hard that he dropped to his knees and let out a howl of pain. 'Crom brought a HUMAN to MY COURT?' he roared, right in Crom's ear.

'Forgive Crom, my king . . .' whimpered Crom.

But Tull twisted even harder, until Crom roared in agony, beating his hand on the ground in submission.

Which was when a voice rang out: the voice of a tiny human boy.

'Leave him alone!'

Tull released Crom's ear, Crom collapsing to the floor with a groan. Then Tull turned back to see Marcus, fists clenched, perched high on the seat of the throne.

There was a long silence.

Then, one by one, the giants began to laugh.

'And who is going to make me –' Tull grinned, playing to the crowd – 'little human boy?'

The giants were now falling off their seats laughing, tears rolling down their cheeks.

'Sorry, no, I just . . .' began Marcus. He needed to think of something, fast. 'You didn't let Crom finish. It seems only fair to point out that after I helped him get free, he kidnapped me. He brought me here to . . .' Marcus racked his brains. 'To help! To help you find the king.'

Tull nodded slowly, as if absorbing the information. 'Hmm.' He narrowed his eyes. 'Is this true?' he asked Crom.

Crom nodded sheepishly, playing along.

Tull drew in a deep intake of breath.

'So, where is the king?'

'Um, in London,' said Marcus. 'The capital.'

'The capital,' repeated Tull. 'What is capital?'

'That's where the government is, where the country is run from,' explained Marcus.

'What is a government?' asked Tull.

Marcus blew out his cheeks in a huge sigh. What a day! 'Well, it's, um, the prime minister is head of the government, and the country votes for them, and then they run the country.'

Tull frowned. 'So who is leader?'

Marcus thought for a moment. 'Well, we have a king and a prime minister.'

'But king is in charge?'

'Well, no, we have a parliamentary democracy, so it's really the prime minister.'

There were murmurs of confusion among the giants, Tull holding up his hand to silence them.

'Then what does king do?'

'Well, he . . . um . . . well, he's an important, you know, figure . . .' said Marcus.

'But he's not in charge?'

'Not exactly.'

More mutterings. Tull frowned.

'So why doesn't he kill the prime minister and take charge?'

'Well, that's not how things are decided here.'

'How are they decided?'

'Well, people talk, and—'

'*TALK??*'

The giants again fell about laughing at this, as if it was the funniest thing they had ever heard.

'They *talk?*'

The same giant that had retched at Marcus's stink was now almost sick with laughter.

'So where does this prime minister live?'

'Er, well . . .' said Marcus, stalling for time. He bit his lip, thinking hard. What was he to do? If he told Tull the answer, he'd be putting millions of people in danger. If he didn't, his and Crom's lives were almost certainly over.

'Let's see if Tull can squeeze it out of you.' Tull smiled, cruelty flashing in his eyes.

Marcus gulped as the king's finger and thumb began to close in on him.

'Wait!' shouted Marcus.

He had to tell, and figure the rest out later.

'Downing Street. That way!' yelled Marcus, pointing. 'Down this road, all the way to London, then follow the river . . . past Big Ben – opposite the big wheel. You can't miss it.'

'Fine. We'll go to his house – then the king's – and we'll have a good TALK with both of them,' announced Tull to the giants, who fell about laughing. 'Then we'll TALK to all the other humans too . . .'

The giants were crying and slapping each other on the back.

'One by one!' continued the Giant King. 'Starting . . . with . . . you!'

Tull suddenly made a lunge for Marcus, but just as his fingers were closing around him, another hand snatched him up.

It was Crom.

There was a tense silence, as if Crom had been acting on instinct and was now terrified.

Tull rose to his full, terrible height.

'You dare to challenge your king?' he bellowed.

Crom hung his head.

'Wish to be king in my place, do you?'

'No, sire,' stuttered Crom, stumbling back towards his bench, placing Marcus carefully on his own seat. 'Just to keep boy safe, in case—'

But Tull wasn't listening. 'Come on then! You know the rules. You must defeat me first!'

Crom began to tremble, avoiding Tull's eye. 'In case we might, umm, need his help later, or if we get lost, or . . .'

Tull's eyes twitched as he made a swift mental calculation. Crom, he seemed to decide, had a point. 'Fine,' he spat. 'Crom can keep stupid human for now, but once we've found the capital, he's MINE.'

'So let's go!' called one of the giants.

'To the capital!'

'Kill the king!' chorused another.

'You mean the prime minister,' said another voice.

'Oh yeah,' replied the earlier giant. 'Forgot.'

'NO!'

Tull's voice rang out across the Court of the Giant King, and the giants fell silent.

'Giants wait. The sky is already getting light. Giants don't want to be seen. Tomorrow we fight, take them by surprise. Humans won't know what hit them.'

A ripple of evil laughter rang out from the sitting giants.

'Back to your mounds, to sleep,' declared Tull.

'Giants wake again tomorrow – at midnight!'

'Tomorrow, at midnight!' chorused the giants.

'THEN we meet here,' he said, 'and we march –
to the capital!'

'TO THE CAPITAL!'

CHAPTER SIXTEEN

Marcus felt a wave of relief as, one by one, the giants stalked out of the stone circle and off to their mounds, their vast bodies silhouetted against the grey pre-dawn sky.

Only Crom stayed put, staring down at his feet.

'Are you okay?' asked Marcus.

There was a pause.

'You're not going to do this, are you, Crom?'

Crom didn't answer. Instead, he scooped Marcus up, placed him on his shoulder and began walking back across the plain in the direction they'd come from.

'You can't just kill everyone!' blurted Marcus. 'You have to talk to the other giants! Make them see sense!'

'I am not the king,' said Crom sullenly. 'The king decides.'

'Look,' pleaded Marcus as they reached the main road. 'I know change is difficult, I know you're angry . . . but you can't just destroy the world because you don't like it! There are good things in the new world too! Lights mean people can see in the dark . . . Roads allow families to visit each other more easily . . . or get to hospital quickly if they're sick! And you liked the music, didn't you?'

But Crom seemed not to hear him. Instead, he kept walking, pausing only to check right and left as he crossed the tarmac. Soon they were back in the field where they'd started. Marcus could see the downed pylon, fizzing in the darkness between them and Merlin's. Time was running out.

'Look,' said Marcus, thinking fast. 'Not all humans are bad, I promise. We've cut down trees, I know, but we've done good things too . . . We put a man on the moon!'

Crom frowned. 'To punish him?'

'No! To explore. And we've climbed Everest . . .' Confusion flashed across Crom's face. 'It's a mountain. And cars! You saw how fast they go. They're pretty cool, right? Humans have done lots of great things . . . Do they really all deserve to die?'

But it was no use. 'Giants do as Giant King says,' Crom muttered as he stepped back over the elm trees into the school grounds, adding, 'I'm sorry.'

Soon they were back at the mound; or at least, back in the place where the mound had once been.

Setting Marcus down gently on the courtyard paving stones, Crom settled himself into position, turning this way and that, until he was satisfied he was exactly in place. Then somehow, like an octopus mimicking an outcrop of coral, he began to transform himself, his massive frame contorting until once again he resembled a grassy mound, crowned by hawthorn bushes and ancient gnarled trees, with a neat spiral path and a flagpole standing proudly on top, as if announcing the giant's return to the earth.

Marcus steeled himself.

'Fine,' he said. 'I'll stop them on my own.'

He was just turning to leave when his foot struck something man-made.

The megaphone!

And there was the staff, just a few feet away. He had to return them!

They had both taken a bit of a battering. Somehow, he would have to get them cleaned up; on top of everything else he had to do today – like save humanity – he didn't really feel like being expelled any more.

Taking one last look at the mound, he pushed

back in through the double doors, easing them shut behind him as quietly as he could, and . . .

His heart stopped.

Standing in the corridor, awake and waiting, was Mr Sheen.

CHAPTER SEVENTEEN

'Where have you been?' asked Mr Sheen. 'Rex woke me, said you weren't in your bed. We've been worried.'

'Something terrible has happened – we're . . . we're all in danger!' blurted Marcus.

'What have you got there?' said Mr Sheen, frowning. 'Is that . . . ?'

'Yes, I'm sorry. I took the cloak and staff and . . .'

'From my office?' Mr Sheen sounded shocked and hurt.

'Yes, I'm sorry, but I took them to the mound, and I woke the giant . . .'

Mr Sheen raised his eyebrows. 'The giant?'

'Yes, the mound woke up and became a giant . . .'

The headteacher glanced out of the window. 'That mound?'

'Yes. He's gone back to sleep now, but you have to believe me. It's not just him . . . There are others, and they're angry, about Merlin, about the trees, and they're going to march to the capital – they're going to—'

Mr Sheen held up a hand, cutting Marcus off, and looked at him with concern. 'You know those are just stories, don't you? Merlin, and giants . . .' He paused, trying to find the right words. 'It's just a bit of fun. It's meant to provoke

149

your imaginations. It's not real.'

'It IS real!' shouted Marcus. 'I've seen them!'

'Uh-huh,' said Mr Sheen. 'May I?' he said, reaching out a hand.

Marcus looked down at the broken staff. With a flash of guilt, he remembered how much he had wanted to upset Mr Sheen. Judging from the teacher's expression, he had succeeded.

'I'm sorry,' said Marcus, handing the staff over, along with the megaphone and scrunched-up cloak, and looking at the ground. 'I wanted to make you angry so that you kicked me out, but . . . I don't want that now. I just want . . .'

Mr Sheen shook his head sadly. 'Go through to my office,' he said. 'I'll get us a hot drink. You look cold. I'll see you in there in a moment.'

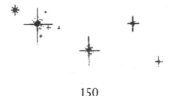

The minutes that Marcus spent in Mr Sheen's office waiting for him to return were torture. He couldn't bear the sight of the empty cabinet where the staff should have been, the desk he had stolen the keys from, the missing cloak and megaphone. It felt as if the room itself was criticizing him, reminding him what he had done wrong.

Not that any of that mattered now.

The most important thing was to stop the giants. There had to be a way . . .

The door opened, and Marcus spun to face the headteacher.

'We have to stop them!' he blurted.

Mr Sheen frowned and passed him the hot drink.

Marcus took a deep breath. 'Look, I'm sorry,' he said. 'I haven't explained this very well. Let me try again.'

'I'm listening,' said Mr Sheen.

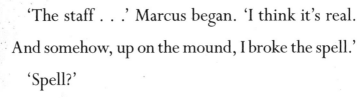

'The staff . . .' Marcus began. 'I think it's real. And somehow, up on the mound, I broke the spell.'

'Spell?'

'The one that Merlin put on the giants. Maybe because the stone fell out . . . The green stone. I think that's what gave the staff its magic.'

'Marcus, these are just stories.'

'No!' said Marcus. 'Well, actually, yes, that story, about the giants being defeated by King Arthur, it's not true. Actually the giants won, but Merlin tricked them and that's why they're so angry.'

'There's a useful expression, coined by the astronomer, Carl Sagan. Have you ever heard of him?'

Marcus shook his head.

'You should look him up sometime. He was also fascinated by the idea of creatures from other worlds – aliens, in his case. But as he put it: *extraordinary claims require extraordinary evidence.*'

'I've got evidence!' insisted Marcus, pointing at the painting. 'Stonehenge. How do you think it was made?'

'No one knows.'

'Giants built it!' exclaimed Marcus triumphantly. 'The tall arch in the middle, that's where their king sits – that's his throne. And the rest of the giants, they sit round the edge. Think about it: humans could never move stones that big without cranes and stuff. Stonehenge is proof that giants exist!'

'That's not evidence. That's conjecture,' said Mr Sheen. 'It's a theory. A rather lovely one, but a fanciful one, all the same.'

'I saw them!' insisted Marcus. 'Anyway, the point is, they're going to march on London tonight,

153

kill the prime minister first, and then the king, and then everybody else, so they can take back the land. We have to do something!'

Mr Sheen took a sip of his hot chocolate as his phone pinged.

'That's your mum,' he said, putting the phone down. 'She's on her way.'

'My mum?'

Mr Sheen looked at him. 'You really have the most extraordinary imagination, Marcus. And I hope one day you put it to good use.'

As he swirled the dregs of his hot chocolate and took the final swig, the penny dropped.

'You're kicking me out!'

'For whatever reason, Marcus, this environment has not been good for you. This is as much a source of regret for me as I'm sure it will be for you, and I wish there was more I could do. But I cannot have you going out alone at night — we are responsible for you. Go and get your things together, please. Quietly. Your fellow students are still asleep.'

'But . . .' began Marcus, his mouth opening and closing like a floundering fish. 'No one gets kicked out of Merlin's!'

'Well —' Mr Sheen sighed, rising to his feet — 'there's a first time for everything.'

By the time Marcus's mum arrived, the birds were singing and the sun was climbing in the morning sky. She gave Marcus a hug.

'Is Dad . . . ?' asked Marcus, looking over at the car hopefully.

'I don't know where your dad is, Marcus,' said his mum with a note of exasperation. 'He isn't answering his phone, as usual.'

An invisible hand reached into Marcus's chest and squeezed his heart.

'Come on,' said his mum gently. 'Let's get you home.'

Marcus took a last look back at Merlin's, at the mound that at this moment only he knew was actually a sleeping giant.

'Psssst!'

Marcus looked around.

'Psssst!'

There it was again. Then he spotted him. It was Rex, hiding in the bushes.

Marcus rushed over to him while his mum searched for her keys.

'I'm sorry,' hissed Rex. 'I didn't want to get you in trouble. I mean, I know you *wanted* to get in trouble . . . but I was just worried about you because you didn't come back.'

'It doesn't matter. I'm not angry,' said Marcus. 'Listen, I need you to do something for me.'

'Marcus?' His mum was calling from the car.

'Look, this is going to sound crazy, but the mound . . .' began Marcus. 'Well, it's a giant. And tonight, when everyone's asleep, it's going to wake up and join all the other giants at Stonehenge, and march to London and . . .'

'Marcus!' There was anger in his mum's voice. 'What are you doing?'

'You don't have to believe me now,' said Marcus. 'I know you think I'm mad, or lying, or both – that's fine – but just please do one thing for me –' he grabbed his friend by the shoulders and looked him square in the eye – 'just please stay awake tonight, and watch the mound, and see for yourself . . .'

'Marcus, come on!' called his mum.

157

'Please?' begged Marcus. 'And tell Tilly I'm sorry for pushing her. And that I'm really glad she's okay.'

Rex's mouth opened and closed, but no words came out.

With one last desperate look back at Rex, Marcus got into the car.

CHAPTER EIGHTEEN

When Marcus got home, he went up to his room and collapsed on his bed, broken. He'd been lying there ever since, redialling his dad's number over and over again. What else was there to do?

The world was ending, no one believed him, and there was nothing he could do about it.

He'd been thrown out of Merlin's – the only child in history, it seemed, to have achieved that –

which now meant he was going to be expelled. Once, he would have been proud of that fact – it was what he'd wanted, after all – but now all he could think was that he had stolen from someone who was trying to help him, and he had hurt and let down his new friends.

Plus, did he mention the world was ending?

His phone rang and Marcus leaped at it. 'Dad!' he yelled. 'I've been trying to get hold of you all day . . .'

'Son of mine!' came the answer. 'Sorry I couldn't answer before. Important meeting. What can I do you for?'

'Right,' said Marcus. 'Where are you?'

'It's this crazy schedule I'm on. I was up in Cambridge this morning, Harlow at lunchtime – I was going to try and squeeze in Wembley when it all kicked off in Peterborough. What's the problem? You're not worried about this Merlin's thing, are you?'

'Err no, it's something else.'

But his dad wasn't listening.

'Don't worry about it. I had a look at the website. That headmaster – whatshisname, Sheen – looks like a right crackpot. You're better off out of it.'

'Dad, it's something else,' pressed Marcus.

'He dresses up as a wizard – did you know that?'

'Dad, this is serious – giants are going to attack London.'

There was a pause.

'Could you say that again?'

'I said *giants are going to attack London.*'

His dad snorted with laughter. 'Sorry, mate, I thought you said *giants are going to attack London* . . . I love it when someone says something, and someone else thinks they've said something

161

different, especially if what they *think* they've heard is something silly. Kills me, it really does.'

There was the sound of a lorry passing.

'Look, sorry mate, I've gotta go. I'll call you later!'

And the line went dead. Marcus hung up. This was hopeless. No one was ever going to believe him.

There was a little knock on the door.

'Go away!' Marcus yelled, flinging his phone on the floor and lying back on the bed.

But the door creaked open anyway, and a tiny pigtailed head popped round it.

'Hi,' said Minnie. 'I brought you a snack.'

'I'm not hungry,' said Marcus.

'It's apple,' she added. 'With peanut butter. You have to try it.'

Marcus didn't answer. He didn't move.

Minnie crept into the room and set the tray

down on his bedside table.

'Daddy says you saw giants.'

Marcus sat up and looked at her.

'What were they like?' she asked, blinking up at him, her eyes wide with hope.

'So, you believe me?' he said.

Minnie nodded enthusiastically. 'Course,' she said, and took a slice of apple. Then she sat on the end of his bed, waiting to hear more.

'One of them, Crom, he was really nice.'

'How tall was he?'

Marcus pulled a face. 'Really tall.'

'Bigger than a tree?'

'Much bigger. So big, he got his arm stuck in a pylon,' said Marcus, and Minnie laughed.

'I wish I could meet a giant,' she said, helping herself to another slice of Marcus's apple, dipping it carefully in the dob of peanut butter. 'You've got

163

to try this,' she said. 'It's amazing.'

Marcus took a bite. She was right – it was delicious: shivery-sour apple mixed with salty-sweet peanut butter.

'What are the other giants like?' asked Minnie.

Marcus frowned.

'Are they bad?' she asked.

After a moment, Marcus said, 'Some of them. They want to attack London.'

'So, what are you going to do?'

Marcus sighed. 'I don't know. No one will listen – no one believes me – and I can hardly defeat a bunch of giants on my own.'

'Daddy will listen,' said Minnie firmly. 'Maybe you can go after them in one of his planes?'

Marcus let out a little snort of laughter.

'Colin doesn't fly planes, Minnie,' said Marcus. 'He's just a tour guide.'

'Minnie!' called Marcus's mum from out on the landing. 'It's bedtime.'

Minnie glanced at the door to check no one was coming in. Then she whispered, 'They fly them too.'

'Where are you?' called his mum again.

'In Marcus's room!' called Minnie, getting up to leave.

'Wait,' said Marcus, catching hold of her sleeve. 'What do you mean?'

'Shh!' said Minnie, holding her finger to her lips and whispering. 'It's a secret.'

Which was when Marcus's mum popped her head around the door.

'Oh,' she said, surprised to find Marcus and Minnie together.

'We were just saying goodnight,' said Minnie, smiling sweetly.

'Goodness,' said Marcus's mum, pleased. 'In that case, Marcus, maybe you'd like to read Minnie her bedtime story?'

Marcus glanced at Minnie, then at his mum. 'I'd love to,' he replied.

'Come on,' said Marcus impatiently. 'Tell me please.'

'Tell you what?' replied Minnie innocently, flicking through the books on the shelf in her bedroom.

Marcus rolled his eyes. He was beginning to lose patience. They had already wasted endless amounts of time cleaning Minnie's teeth, then filling her unicorn hot-water bottle, then fetching her a glass of water to go beside her bed, then watching her do gymnastics on her bedroom rug, then making her a hot chocolate, then cleaning her teeth again, and Marcus was desperate to move things on.

'About the planes!' pressed Marcus, standing up from the bed.

'Oh, yes,' said Minnie, handing him a book. 'The planes. The thing is . . .' She paused as she clambered up on to the bed and underneath the covers. 'Your mum's not supposed to know, and any minute now, she'll come in to check on me. So why don't you read to me for a bit – then when she's gone, I'll tell you.'

Minnie smiled winningly, patting the duvet beside her.

Reluctantly, Marcus sat back down.

'Fine,' he said huffily, opening the cover.

As he did, a photo fell out, on to the duvet.

Marcus picked it up: it showed Minnie as a baby, Colin and a pretty dark-haired lady, who he guessed must be Minnie's mum. They were all sitting in Betsy, Colin's beat-up old car, smiling at the camera, as if they were about to head off on a journey.

He smiled, handing the photo back to Minnie, who put it carefully between the pages.

Marcus felt a pang of sympathy. Minnie's mum had died when Minnie was very small. She seemed happy enough now, but Minnie must have been through a lot.

Marcus decided a bedtime story was the least he could give her.

'Well, this is a sight for sore eyes,' said his mum, creeping in just as he got to the end. 'Now have you kissed your daddy goodnight?'

Minnie nodded.

'Good. Then here's a kiss from me . . .' Marcus's mum leaned over, kissing Minnie on the forehead. 'I'm completely washed out,' she said, kissing Marcus on the head too. 'I'm going to get an early night. And, Marcus, straight to bed yourself, afterwards, please: it's late. Let's all have a better day tomorrow, shall we?'

The door closed followed by silence. The coast was clear.

'Right,' whispered Marcus. 'Now, one last time. What's all this about planes?'

CHAPTER NINETEEN

Marcus lay in his bed, tossing and turning, going over and over what Minnie had just told him.

'Dad flies the planes. At the museum. They all do.'

It couldn't be true, could it?

Minnie had said that Colin had kept it from his mum because he hadn't wanted to worry her.

Yes, it was possible. His mum had hated his dad's motorbike, going on and on about how they

weren't safe. If she knew Colin was flying antique planes, she would almost certainly freak.

Marcus glanced at his bedside clock: 9.35 p.m.

In just a few hours, the giants would be waking up.

Throwing back the covers, he padded over to his bedroom window and pulled back the curtain. Silver light seeped into the room, the moon a bright circle behind stormy clouds.

Below him, surrounded by a high wooden fence, lay their tiny back garden. At its far end, framed in the bright window of the garden shed, was Colin.

Marcus shook his head. Two arguments were

struggling against each other inside him.

On the one hand – his mum's new boyfriend was a massive dweeb.

On the other hand – the end of the world, etc. And somehow Marcus knew Minnie would be right about one thing – Colin would at least listen.

He glanced back at the clock.

9.40 p.m.

Marcus took a deep breath, slipped on his trainers, and crept down the stairs and out the back door, into the garden.

Wrapping his dressing gown tightly around him, he picked his way across the damp grass and knocked on the door of the shed.

Colin threw open the door.

'Marcus!' he said in surprise. 'Here, come in – it's freezing.'

Marcus nodded and stepped inside, Colin

closing the door behind him.

'There's a bad storm coming, according to the news.'

Marcus nodded again. 'What *is* that?' he asked, pointing at the greasy object in Colin's hands.

'Th-this?' said Colin, so happy that Marcus was talking to him that he stumbled on his words. 'Oh, you know, the usual,' said Colin with a shrug.

'Betsy?' asked Marcus.

Colin nodded. 'Should be sorted now.'

'I don't know why you don't just dump that old rust bucket,' said Marcus.

'Well, Minnie's mum was rather fond of the old girl,' said Colin, 'and I just haven't quite got the heart to give up on her.'

Marcus's cheeks flushed with shame. He'd had no idea. Colin's dedication made a bit more sense now. Marcus suddenly felt lost for words.

Colin looked up at him. 'Are you okay? Quite a day you've had.'

'I know no one believes me,' Marcus said. 'About the giants.'

'Well, Marcus,' began Colin, 'it *is* a rather extraordinary claim.'

Suddenly Mr Sheen's words popped into Marcus's head.

'Have you heard the expression, *Extraordinary claims require*—?'

'*Extraordinary evidence*,' finished Colin.

'So what if I was to show you some?' asked Marcus. 'Evidence, that is.'

There was a pause.

'Go on,' said Colin.

'The thing is . . .' said Marcus. 'We'd need a plane. And I don't know where we'd get one of those – do you?'

Colin studied Marcus carefully.

'Who have you been talking to?' he asked.

'Minnie,' said Marcus. 'In strictest confidence, of course.'

There was another pause.

'She said you fly the planes. At the museum. But I didn't believe her.'

Colin narrowed his eyes. 'You don't, eh?'

'But then,' Marcus continued, glancing at his watch, 'you don't believe me that at midnight a bunch of angry giants are going to rise up and march on Downing Street, do you?'

Colin eyed him carefully. 'Well,' he said, standing and wiping his greasy hands on his trousers, 'I guess there's only one way to find out.'

CHAPTER TWENTY

I t wasn't the smoothest of getaways.

'Are you sure we shouldn't just take Mum's car?' said Marcus. 'You know, just in case . . .'

He didn't want to make a big deal out of it, but this was rather a life-and-death emergency situation and Marcus wasn't convinced Betsy was up to the job, whatever her sentimental value.

'No, no,' said Colin as they huddled under the

open bonnet of the 2CV, 'it'll be fine. If you just point the torch down here, I'll try and get this thing in place.'

But the part wouldn't seem to slot in where it was meant to.

'The thread won't catch,' murmured Colin, examining it closely. 'My fingers are too big to turn it properly. I don't suppose you could . . . ?'

'Give it here,' hissed Marcus impatiently.

Handing the torch to Colin, he lined up the part carefully, screwing it tight.

'Oh, bravo!' exclaimed Colin a little too loudly.

A light flipped on in the upstairs window.

'Shh, Mum's awake!'

'Don't worry,' whispered Colin. 'She's probably just going to the loo. Come on.'

As quietly as they could, the two of them climbed into the front seat of the 2CV.

'We'd better wait,' warned Marcus. 'Until her light goes off.'

For a few moments, the two of them sat in Colin's old car, staring up at the windows of the house, waiting.

'Look, Marcus . . .' began Colin in a whisper.

Marcus looked at him warily.

'I know you and I haven't always seen eye to eye . . . I just want you to know, I'm not trying to replace your dad. I just . . . I just like your mum, and I think she likes me, at least I hope she does, since we're getting married. But anyway . . . the point is, your dad will always be your dad and—'

'It's out,' said Marcus, pointing to the bedroom window.

'Right,' said Colin awkwardly. 'Good, well . . .'

He turned the ignition key, and the

engine chugged into life!

'YES!' exclaimed Colin at the top of his voice.

Above them, the bedroom light snapped back on, the curtains swishing open to reveal Marcus's mum staring down at them, her mouth rounded in surprise.

Marcus couldn't help laughing. 'You're for it now!' he said.

'Don't worry, I'll handle this,' said Colin, rolling down the window. 'Bye, Abi!' he shouted. 'See you later!'

Then, giving Marcus's mum a wave, as if driving off with Marcus in the middle of the night was the most natural thing in the world, Colin backed down the driveway on to the road.

'Expertly handled,' said Marcus, grinning. 'Though something tells me that might not be the last we'll hear from her.'

As they turned on to the main road, Marcus's phone rang.

'Hi, Mum,' he said.

'Pass me to Colin, please,' came the curt reply.

'It's for you,' said Marcus with a grin, putting the phone on speaker.

'What's going on? Where are you going? Are you with Marcus?'

'Yes, love,' replied Colin. 'We're just going for a drive.'

'Do you know what time it is?'

'There's something we have to do.'

'It's the middle of the night!'

'Well, it's rather time sensitive . . .'

There was a pause, Marcus stifling a smile.

'This doesn't concern Marcus's stupid story about the giants marching on Downing Street, does it?'

'Look, love,' replied Colin, 'he really seems like he's telling the truth . . .'

'THAT A BUNCH OF GIANTS ARE ABOUT TO DESTROY THE HUMAN RACE???'

'Well, either way, we're just going to pop down there, make sure nothing untoward is happening . . .'

'What – you're going to drive to Downing Street? Now?'

Marcus looked at Colin with raised eyebrows, watching to see if he would put his mum straight.

'Like I say, I'm sure it'll be nothing and we'll be back home in a jiffy.'

'But London's miles away. How are you going to . . . ?'

'Uh-oh,' said Colin, as if he was auditioning for a part as the world's worst actor ever. 'I'm losing you. Must be bad reception – bye . . .'

And then he hung up.

'You're toast when she finds out,' said Marcus, enjoying someone else being in trouble for once.

'Well, I suppose it doesn't matter if giants are going to wipe us all out before sunrise, does it?' said Colin.

He caught Marcus's eye and grinned. Then he stepped hard on the accelerator.

For a pram on wheels, Betsy really could move. Soon they were bouncing over speed bumps, rattling around roundabouts, and juddering along main roads, out into open countryside, heading for the air museum.

'So it's true?' asked Marcus. 'What Minnie said? About you flying the planes?'

Colin shot him a sideways glance.

'It's not just me,' replied Colin mischievously. 'We all do. Bolu started it, the lady who runs the tea shop. Decided to get her pilot's licence. She took us up, one by one, and we all got the bug. I'd always loved planes, since I was a little boy. I just always saw myself more as a spotter, a fixer, an *enthusiast*, rather than a pilot.'

'No kidding,' said Marcus drily.

'We call ourselves the Teatime Assortment in her honour.' Colin grinned.

'Why did you never tell Mum?' asked Marcus.

There was a guilty pause.

'I don't know,' said Colin with a sigh. 'I didn't want to worry her, I suppose. She always said your dad buying that motorbike was the end, the final straw. She thought it was show-offy, dangerous. She was convinced he was going to have an accident. So it seemed best not to mention it.'

He glanced at Marcus, looking for reassurance that he was doing the right thing. But Marcus tutted.

'Bad move,' said Marcus. 'You've got to come clean. Take it from me, if there's one thing Mum hates, it's someone lying to her. Mum and I, we've got this rule,' Marcus continued. 'So long as I own up, I'm never in trouble.'

'Hmmm,' said Colin thoughtfully.

'So do it,' concluded Marcus. 'Own up.'

Colin nodded slowly. 'Well, thank you, Marcus,' he said sincerely. 'I appreciate your thoughts on this, especially given . . . well, you know.'

Of course, it hadn't escaped Marcus's attention that he now had the perfect way to get rid of Colin . . .

I mean, what if his mum found out that her new partner had been lying to her for ages *before* he'd had the chance to own up? That wouldn't go down well at all . . .

But Marcus put the thought out of his mind for

now as Colin pulled the car up outside a chain-linked gate, leaned out through the driver's window to punch a number into a keypad and, as the gate swung slowly open, drove them suavely through.

Colin grinned. 'Welcome to Guildford Air Museum.'

CHAPTER TWENTY-ONE

Colin turned in his seat to face Marcus, eyes twinkling. 'No cameras at this entrance, so no one will ever know we were here.'

'Wait, so the museum doesn't know you fly the planes either?' said Marcus.

'Well, they do,' said Colin, 'but they generally need a bit of notice and perhaps a slightly more solid reason than to investigate the fantasies of a ten-year-old boy.' Marcus gave him a look. 'Which may well turn out to be true!'

Soon they were speeding across a vast airfield, giant hangars looming in the darkness.

'That's good,' said Colin as they passed a windsock rippling in a stiff wind. 'We'll have the wind with us.'

He pulled to halt outside the museum hangar and, leaving the car headlights on so they could see, leaped out. At the hangar doors, Colin punched in another combination, then vanished inside.

A moment later a vast metal door rolled upwards. Marcus gasping as a brightly lit museum space full of old planes was slowly revealed.

'You can turn Betsy's lights off now,' called Colin.

Marcus did as instructed, then walked over to the hangar to find Colin climbing up into a yellow biplane, flicking switches and making adjustments.

'The Tiger Moth!' exclaimed Marcus. 'From the Battle of Britain?'

'So you *were* listening,' said Colin over his shoulder.

'Is it safe to fly?' asked Marcus uncertainly. 'Even in a storm?'

'Heavens, no!' said Colin, jumping back down. 'It's madness.'

'Um,' said Marcus. 'Okay. Are you sure we should—?'

'Here.' Colin handed Marcus a crash helmet, and helped him fasten the strap under his chin. 'Now we'll be able to hear each other.'

Then he reached up and yanked on the propeller, which immediately began to spin, creating a deafening noise.

'So far, so good,' said Colin, his tinny voice

coming through on a speaker beside Marcus's ear. 'While I bring her out of the hangar, can you go into the air traffic control cabin and turn on the runway lights?'

'Er, which one's that?' asked Marcus, slightly alarmed at the responsibility.

'The tall one,' replied Colin. 'Big windows, red and white – you can't miss it.'

Swallowing hard, Marcus sprinted out to the only red-and-white building he could see, threw open the door and rushed up the stairs. There were switches and controls everywhere!

'Runway lights, runway lights . . . There!' he said, spotting the correct controls at last.

He threw the switch and gasped. Twinkling lights appeared all along the length of the runway.

Racing back downstairs, he saw Colin driving past the cabin in the plane.

'Climb up!' Colin said.

'Er, I will if you stop moving!' replied Marcus, trying to keep up.

'Sorry,' said Colin. 'No brakes. This is as slow as she goes. Run along behind us, climb up onto the wing, and into the front seat.'

'Are you serious?'

'And try not to get caught in the propeller,' replied Colin.

Marcus raised his eyebrows in surprise, but there was no time to argue, so he did as he was told, hauling himself up into the lower wing, then edging along a marked walkway, and into the front seat. The mixture of wood and cloth that formed the body of the plane seemed very flimsy, and the only nod to comfort was the leather on the not-very-padded seat. As he fastened the flight harness, it dawned on Marcus that a Tiger Moth was basically a go-kart with wings.

'Ready?' said Colin. 'Buckle up!'

And with that, Colin opened the throttle. The engine roared and thrust them forward. Marcus closed his eyes as the entire plane began to shake so hard he wondered if it might actually explode. Then, as they reached maximum speed, Colin pulled back on the joystick, the ground fell away, and they were airborne.

Higher and higher they climbed, the engine straining, the runway lights falling away behind them. Then, with the airfield just one square in a patchwork of fields, Colin levelled her off. Marcus marvelled at the beautiful sight stretching out below him: the pretty lights of their hometown, and other further-away towns, and the roads that linked them, all twinkling away like stars.

'Wow,' said Marcus. He looked across at Colin, who grinned.

'So,' said Colin, 'do you have a plan for how we're going to defeat these giants, should we happen to find any?'

'As a matter of fact,' said Marcus, pulling out his phone, 'I do.'

CHAPTER TWENTY-TWO

'What time is it?' whispered Rex. 'Quarter to midnight,' replied Tilly with a yawn.

The two friends were sitting in front of the big window at the top of the stairs, wrapped in blankets, eyes fixed on the mound.

'Come on,' urged Rex, 'it's not much longer now. Then we can go back to bed.'

There was a long pause, broken only by the

sound of a tawny owl, calling in the night.

'Do you think there's any chance Marcus is telling the truth?' said Tilly.

'I don't know,' said Rex. 'He was in a bit of a state, to be honest . . .' His voice trailed away as he remembered the expression in Marcus's eyes that morning outside school. 'Kicked out of Merlin's. Poor guy.'

Just then, Tilly's phone rang. Rex and Tilly looked at each other.

'It's him,' confirmed Tilly as she took the call.

'Tilly?' asked Marcus, his voice battling the wind. 'Did I wake you?'

'Course not, silly. I'm with Rex, watching the mound, like you asked.'

'Seriously?' Marcus felt a lump in his throat. 'You did that for me? I . . . I don't know what to say . . .'

For a moment, Marcus was genuinely lost for words.

'Where are you?' asked Tilly. 'It sounds very noisy.'

'In a plane,' replied Marcus. 'A Tiger Moth, to be precise. We just took off from Guildford Air Museum.'

'A plane?' repeated Tilly, glancing at Rex and raising her eyebrows.

'Yes. Listen . . . I need to ask you a favour.'

'Okay . . .'

'I need you to wake Mr Sheen . . .'

'Right . . .' replied Tilly uncertainly.

'Tell him to fetch Merlin's cloak and staff, and the megaphone, and drive them to Westminster Bridge, okay?'

'Er, I'm not sure if he's going to be up for doing that, Marcus,' said Tilly, making a *this guy's crazy* face at Rex.

'Well he won't be NOW, obviously!' said Marcus. 'After he's seen the giant, I mean. Just make sure he's watching at midnight too . . . Can you do that? The thing is, Merlin is the only thing the giants are scared of,' continued Marcus. 'It's the only way we can stop them. They're going to attack Downing Street first, then Buckingham Palace. They'll be coming into London along the river, so we'll head them off at the bridge. We'll get there first because we're in the plane, so just . . . get there as quick as you can.'

'Okay, bye. Here's Rex!' said Tilly, shaking her head as she passed the phone over.

'Marcus, it's Rex, um . . .'

'Look, I get it,' said Marcus. 'You don't believe me. Just wake up Mr Sheen, and make sure you're all looking at the mound at midnight, okay? Then, when you realize I'm telling the truth, take the cloak, the staff and the megaphone, and meet me at Westminster Bridge. And . . . thank you. You're . . .' He paused. 'Good friends, both of you. I owe you.'

Then he hung up.

'What time is it?' asked Mr Sheen, appearing in the doorway in his dressing gown.

'Two minutes to midnight,' said Rex apologetically.

'Is everything okay?'

'We're really sorry to wake you,' added Tilly, 'but we just had a call from Marcus.'

'I see,' said Mr Sheen, yawning. His hair was sticking up as if he had just put his finger in an electric socket. 'Giants, is it?'

'Precisely, sir,' said Rex. 'He's asked if we could all please just be watching the mound at midnight. Then, um, he needs us to bring the cloak and staff and megaphone to Westminster Bridge,' he added, awkwardly, 'so he can, you know, stop the giants.'

Rex looked at his feet. Tilly smiled and shrugged.

Mr Sheen sighed. 'I know it's hard when a friend leaves,' he began. 'Especially a friend in distress. It can bring up some difficult emotions. But it's important to understand . . . These stories, about giants and wizards and great magical battles . . . they're legends. Myths. Stories with real power, but they themselves aren't true. Marcus is a bit confused right now. That's why we decided it's best he's with his family.'

Rex and Tilly said nothing.

Mr Sheen stared. 'You don't believe him, do you?' he asked with a tiny laugh.

'Umm,' said Rex.

'Well,' said Tilly.

Neither were quite sure what to say.

'It's not that we believe him exactly, sir,' said Tilly, struggling to find the right words.

'It's just that we promised we'd be watching at midnight,' added Rex, flicking a quick look at the large ticking clock at the end of the hallway. 'One minute to go . . . Should we . . . ?'

'Just in case . . . ?' added Tilly.

They both made as if to walk back down the corridor to the window.

'Oh, come on!' said Mr Sheen. 'You're not telling me that you seriously believe there's a chance that any minute now that mound out there, in our school grounds, is going to turn into a giant?'

Rex looked at the clock again. 'Um, I don't know, sir, but since there's only –' he glanced at his watch again – 'twenty-five seconds to go now, maybe we should all just . . . ?'

'I mean, isn't it a little fantastical? It's not that I'm not a believer in magical thinking – of course I am. I wouldn't be here if I wasn't – but—'

'Sir, we have to go now!' shouted Tilly.

There was a pause.

'Fine, fine, come on then,' said Mr Sheen, sighing wearily, securing his dressing gown with an extravagant bow. 'I suppose I'm up now, anyway.'

Rex and Tilly rushed back down the corridor to the window, pressing their noses against the glass.

'You're good kids,' said Mr Sheen, ambling along behind them. 'I guess I must have underestimated your young, lively imaginations. The thing is, these legends – Merlin, the giants – it's really just a teaching method. I use it as a tool to . . .'

But as he reached the window, the words died on his lips.

Rex and Tilly were staring open-mouthed, Tilly's phone tumbling from her hand to the floor.

The ground beneath their feet began to shake, rattling the windows and flickering the lights, as

right before their eyes the mound began to rise, higher and higher, blotting out the moon and the stars and the whole night sky, bulldozer-loads of soil raining down to reveal the unmistakable outline of a man; only this man was larger and taller and stronger than any man who had ever lived. In fact, he wasn't a man at all.

He was a giant.

CHAPTER TWENTY-THREE

I t was midnight.

Deep in the darkness of the mound, Crom's mind flickered into life. Smiling contentedly, eyes closed, he flexed his neck and shoulders, a delicious ripple of movement travelling all the way to his toes, wringing his body free of sleep.

He took a deep breath. A restless wind was blowing, and he slowly raised his head, opening his eyes. Before him, a dark grass meadow swished and swayed under enormous mountains of silver-edged cloud.

Then he saw the lights on the horizon – too evenly spaced, too steady to be stars. And he remembered. The boy. The pylons. The court. War. Again.

He sighed wearily, pushed himself up to his full height. Sure enough, in the distance he could see them all at play: the tiny humans in their noisy, foul-smelling cars, scurrying back and forth along the brightly lit road like ants on a trail; and in between, fizzing in the darkness, the parade of ugly pylons, one of them crumpled from his recent fall.

Turning, he jumped in alarm. There was light where he wasn't expecting it. A bright yellow square of see-through material, like ice but impossibly thin and clear, and behind it, three creepy-looking humans pressed up against it, staring up at him.

The biggest of the three pointed at him in alarm; then a moment later, the sound of their excited human voices flew past on the wind as they came scrambling out of their lit-up box and climbed into one of the whizzy things. Its noisy innards exploded into life, its lights blazing as it sped away into the night.

Where was it going?

Oh well. Crom had no time for such questions now. He took another deep breath. Then, setting his jaw, he strode purposefully through the darkness, heading to the court. To war.

CHAPTER TWENTY-FOUR

'There it is!' shouted Colin cheerily, his voice distorting in Marcus's helmet.

The Tiger Moth banked sharply, and Marcus glimpsed the bright lights of a dual carriageway.

'That's the A303!' explained Colin. 'It runs from here all the way to Stonehenge. Shall we take a look?'

Marcus nodded. He glanced anxiously at his

watch. 'It's gone midnight, so they should be there.'

He felt his stomach lurch as the plane plummeted downwards, levelling out to bring them directly above the illuminated road, all four lanes clearly visible beneath them.

'See anything?' asked Colin.

Marcus peered down, heart racing, but all he could see was a few cars and lorries – business as usual. He frowned. Surely the giants should be on their way by now?

'They must be further up,' he said.

'Right you are,' said Colin.

They flew in silence to where the dual carriageway thinned to become a main road. They kept going a bit, but there was still no sign.

'Or maybe we missed them?' said Marcus. He was panicking now.

'No problem,' said Colin, smiling at Marcus.

'Let's give the whole road a sweep as far as Stonehenge, shall we? Just to be safe?'

But there was no sign of the giants anywhere. The stone circle itself was clearly visible as they swooped down, flying so low Marcus wondered if the stones might scrape the underside of the plane, but it became painfully obvious that the giants weren't there either.

'I don't get it,' said Marcus. 'They were going to meet at Stonehenge and march on London, I promise you.'

'What do you want to do now?' asked Colin.

'I don't know,' said Marcus, shaking his head. Was he going mad? Had he imagined the whole thing?

'Well, we've got plenty of fuel,' said Colin, 'so take your time. Seeing things from this height, it's a great way to get . . . I don't know . . . perspective.'

Colin paused, circling round to fly back towards London.

'I know you've got a lot going on, Marcus, what with your dad and everything, and—'

'Oh, don't you start!' exclaimed Marcus.

Which was when Marcus's eye caught a movement, deep in the shadows, to the left of the road, far from the streetlights' glare.

'Colin . . .' He gulped.

'What?'

'They're not on the road,' he said. 'Look . . .'

Colin turned to where Marcus was pointing . . .

Then Marcus's impeccably polite stepfather-to-be swore, really loudly, all the colour draining from his face as he tried to make sense of the image that was now burning itself into his brain: a procession of twenty or more giants, marching steadily towards the capital.

CHAPTER TWENTY-FIVE

'See?' shouted Marcus. 'I told you!'

He didn't WANT to be happy about this – obviously it wasn't good news, all things considered – but it did feel good to know at least one other person had seen what he'd seen and knew he was telling the truth.

The next thing he knew, his phone was ringing.

'Marcus!' shouted Tilly. 'We saw him! We saw the giant!'

'What?' asked Marcus excitedly. 'Where?'

'At the school! Where do you think?'

'He's massive!' shouted Rex.

'Frightfully sorry, Marcus!' called Mr Sheen. 'Had you completely wrong. Hazard of the trade! Don't worry, we've got the staff and everything! And we're on our way!'

'See you on the bridge!' exclaimed Tilly, before hanging up.

Marcus couldn't believe it. 'They're on their way,' he told Colin proudly.

'From where – Merlin's? In a car? They'll be ages . . .'

Marcus frowned. His stepfather had a point.

'We have to slow the giants down somehow, give the others time to get there.'

'We could call the RAF?' suggested Colin eagerly. 'I reckon a fleet of Eurofighter Typhoons could take them out no problem. Or Lockheed Lightnings, maybe, with their superior firepower and handling?'

'No!' said Marcus, surprising himself with the force of his own voice. 'No violence. That's not how we solve this.' Then he added in a quieter voice, 'I don't want Crom getting hurt.'

'Who's Crom?' asked Colin.

'The giant from Merlin's. He's one of the good guys. He's . . . my friend. He saved my life.'

Colin thought for a moment. 'In that case,' he said, his voice sizzling with relish, 'this sounds like a job for the Teatime Assortment!'

'But . . . won't they all be asleep?' asked Marcus doubtfully.

'Quite probably,' said Colin, 'but not for long!' Switching the radio to a different frequency, he pressed a button, cleared his throat, then, in a casual, conversational tone – as if he was the pilot of a commercial jet chatting to a plane full of passengers – he said:

'Malted Milk here, requesting a *High Tea*. Repeat: a *High Tea*. Do you read me, over?'

There was a tense silence.

'Malted Milk?' repeated Marcus, eyebrows raised.

'We're named after our favourite biscuits,' said Colin defensively. 'And mine is a Malted Milk.'

A crackle came from the radio; then it burst into life, a string of voices responding eagerly.

'Ginger Nut is go. Repeat: Ginger Nut is go, over …'

'Jammy Dodger also go, over,' replied another.

'Hobnob is go, over.'

'Jaffa Cake is go! Repeat: Jaffa Cake is go, over!'

Frowning, Colin poked at the button.

'A Jaffa Cake is not a biscuit, Kenneth! We've had this discussion.'

213

A crowd of voices jammed the airwaves.

'It really isn't, you know, Kenny . . .'

'Come on, Kenneth . . .'

'How many times . . .'

'FINE!' Kenneth relented. 'But I want to be something fancy. Like a Bourbon.'

Marcus caught Colin's eye, and tapped his wrist.

'Now pay attention,' said Colin, remembering their mission. 'Our rendezvous is the junction of the M3 and A303, over.'

'Copy that, Malted Milk – Jammy Dodger here. What is our objective, over?'

Colin frowned, searching for the right words.

'Malted Milk to Jammy Dodger. Bit of a weird one: to delay some giants.'

There was a long pause. Eventually, Ginger Nut broke the silence.

'Ginger Nut to Malted Milk,' came the hesitant

reply. 'Do you mean giants, as in tall people, over?'

'Malted Milk to Ginger Nut,' replied Colin. 'That is correct: giants, as in extremely tall, made of soil and sticks and stuff, trying to destroy humankind, over.'

Another pause.

'Jaffa Cake to—' began Kenneth.

'Bourbon,' corrected Colin immediately.

'Bourbon to Malted Milk,' said Old Kenneth, correcting himself. 'Is this a joke, over?'

'Malted Milk to Bourbon,' replied Colin. 'No, this is not a joke. I repeat: this is not a joke. You are about to see something your eyes won't believe. But it *is* real, and they *are* dangerous . . . So don't try anything stupid. We have a plan in place – we just need to hold them up a little . . . create a diversion.'

There was another short pause.

'Copy that, Malted Milk,' said Ginger Nut. 'See you shortly.'

Soon the yellow Tiger Moth was approaching the point where the dual carriageway merged with the motorway. Marcus blinked in disbelief as a string of lights appeared in the skies ahead, banking towards them.

'Watch out!' Colin chuckled. 'Here comes the cavalry!'

Sure enough, four old planes were flying in formation, heading straight towards them!

'That was quick!' said Marcus.

'The Teatime Assortment don't mess about,' said Colin, looping around and waving at his squadron.

Bolu pulled up alongside them in a Spitfire.

She was wearing an old-fashioned sheepskin flying jacket and leather helmet and goggles, complete with a white scarf. 'Ginger Nut to Malted Milk,' crackled the radio. 'Please state number of giants and suggested tactics, over.'

'Malted Milk to Ginger Nut,' replied Colin. 'I don't know, but it's a lot. Over twenty, maybe. Tactics are: wasp at a picnic. Buzz them as close as you dare, and see if you can get them to chase you.'

'Copy that, Malted Milk.'

'Here they come,' said Colin, spotting the dark figures beneath them.

'Holy crumpets,' crackled the radio, which was soon jammed with some very colourful language as the Teatime Assortment set eyes on the procession of dark figures advancing steadily up the road towards them.

The fleet plunged from the skies

'Which one shall we go for?' asked Colin.

Marcus's eyes narrowed as he spotted Tull.

'The one at the front,' replied Marcus. 'He's the leader.'

'Everyone ready?' said Colin.

All four pilots gave the thumbs-up.

Colin opened the throttle, and the fleet plunged from the skies, down into the path of the advancing giants.

CHAPTER TWENTY-SIX

'It's true – it's all true . . .' muttered Mr Sheen for the millionth time that night as he screeched his purple Volkswagen Beetle up the A303 towards London.

PARRRRRRP! went the horn of a car as Mr Sheen careered past, then cut in front of it, dangerously close.

'Um, are you perhaps going a little fast, sir?' asked Rex nervously. The whole car was shaking.

Mr Sheen ignored him completely, as if he hadn't heard him, which he probably hadn't. 'King Arthur, Merlin, the giants . . .' he murmured breathlessly, shaking his head in disbelief. 'It's all true!'

'Look out!' called Rex, turning in his seat to give Tilly an alarmed look.

But Tilly's eyes were fixed on the road ahead, a determined expression on her face.

'That's it, sir – go on!' she shouted as, just in time, Mr Sheen yanked on the steering wheel and they lurched into the fast lane, whizzing past an enormous lorry.

'I knew it!' declared Mr Sheen, flinging them back into the middle lane again. 'Deep down, I always believed. I just never dared hope . . . The Giant of Merlin's Mound! In my school!' His eyes had a wild look. 'What was he made of, do you think? Soil?'

'Looked like it, sir,' agreed Tilly. 'Soil and rock.'

'Maybe some plants,' added Rex. 'Roots and stuff.'

'That's why, then!' declared Mr Sheen excitedly. 'That's why the giants never showed up in any of the images archaeologists had made of the inside of all these mounds. No bones! No bones, because they're made out of the earth itself! The Giants of Albion were made of the earth, from their head to their—'

'AARRGGGH!' yelled Mr Sheen as a colossal foot landed on the road ahead of them.

He yanked the steering wheel and stamped on the brakes.

'AARRGGGH!' yelled Rex and Tilly as the Beetle lurched into a violent spin. Round and round it wheeled, the giant foot whirling closer with each turn, until just as they were about to crash, it suddenly vanished.

'Everyone okay?' asked Mr Sheen as the car at last skidded to a halt. 'What happened?'

'It's a giant!' yelled Rex, peering out of the window. 'Look, it's chasing something!'

Sure enough, a yellow biplane was racing across the neighbouring field, chased by an immense dark figure.

'It must be Marcus!' shouted Tilly. 'He said he was in a plane, remember?'

'What's he doing?' asked Rex in disbelief. 'He's going to get himself killed!'

'Look over there – there's more!' called Mr Sheen as four Second World War planes came into view, swarming in the darkness, the blundering giants lumbering after them, doing their best to catch up.

'Haha! It's a diversion!' exclaimed Mr Sheen, clapping his hands. He started up the car again. 'They're slowing the giants down, to give us time to get to London! Come on, let's go!'

CHAPTER TWENTY-SEVEN

In the starry sky above an ancient circle of stones, five planes performed a wild dance. They swooped and veered, dodged and dived, circled down and soared upwards again, always just out of reach of the enormous grasping hands that pursued them.

Exasperated, the giants roared and snatched at the air, chasing the tiny planes up and down the fields, round and round in dizzying spirals, like children chasing butterflies.

Colin gripped the joystick, aiming the Tiger Moth at one of the giants once more. The giant crouched, trying to evade the oncoming aircraft, and as he did, Colin swooped right down and sped through the giant's legs. How he roared!

'Brilliant!' cried Marcus, clapping his hands with delight. Glancing right and left, he saw other planes carrying out similar manoeuvres: some giants swiping at them in irritation; others chasing after them, trying to catch them.

Only Tull stood still, head on one side, studying the planes' movements in the air.

'Watch out,' said Marcus. 'I think he's on to us.'

'I'm going for him!' Colin announced, banking the plane around for another approach. But as he did, Tull launched himself into the air, reaching out with his right hand.

'Look out!' hollered Marcus.

With Tull's outstretched hand closing in around them, Colin threw every ounce of his weight behind the joystick, flipping the plane sideways and slipping through the giant's fingers!

'Phew!' Marcus gasped, breathing a sigh of relief. 'That was close!'

Enraged, Tull bellowed something at his fellow giants. They all stopped and turned to him.

This time, although the biplane steered only inches from the giant's right ear, it was ignored.

'Enough!' bellowed Tull, spinning on his heels and striding purposefully back towards the road.

'He's not going for it!' Marcus cried. 'He's on to us.'

One by one, the other giants gave up their pursuit of the planes, slowly coming to their senses.

They re-formed their line, continuing their

slow, steady march towards London.

'Malted Milk to Ginger Nut, Jammy Dodger, Hobnob and Jaffa Cake,' said Colin into the radio. 'I mean, Bourbon,' he added, correcting himself. 'The game is up. I repeat: the game is up, over.'

In moments, the Teatime Assortment was back in formation. Bolu pulled up beside them in her Spitfire, speaking urgently into the radio.

'Ginger Nut to Malted Milk. So what's the plan? These giants mean business, over?'

The giants were now directly beneath them, Tull leading the way, striding faster than ever.

'Thank you all, Teatime Assortment. But we'll take it from here,' Colin replied.

'Are you sure, Malted Milk?' asked Kenneth. 'Where are the giants headed?'

'Downing Street,' said Colin. 'We're going to cut them off on Westminster Bridge.'

'But . . . how will you stop them?' Jammy Dodger enquired.

'Let's not worry about the details,' Colin replied. 'The point is, thanks to all of you, Phase One is complete. Phase Two, I'm afraid, must be a solo mission.'

'Not your decision, Malted Milk.'

'We're not leaving you, Malted Milk.'

'Thanks, everyone.' Colin paused, emotion in his voice. 'You are true friends. But I must insist. One plane can slip ahead unnoticed. Not so a fleet. Next round at the canteen is on me. Over.'

There was another pause, the weight of Colin's decision, what was at stake, suddenly bearing heavy on all of them. Then the radio channel crackled back into life, crowded with the Teatime Assortment's upbeat farewells.

'Ginger Nut to Malted Milk: good luck!'

'Jammy Dodger to Malted Milk: knock 'em dead, champ!'

'Hobnob to Malted Milk: God speed, over!'

Only Old Kenneth's voice sounded a note of caution.

'Bourbon to Malted Milk: you are making a huge mistake, over.'

Every pilot in the formation turned their head towards Kenneth, who beamed the broadest of smiles.

'A Jaffa Cake is definitely a biscuit!' he crowed. 'Good luck, both of you!'

Colin gave them a salute; then, with a final wave, the four planes peeled away, following the river towards the bright lights of the city.

For a few minutes Colin and Marcus circled the skies in silence.

Then Colin said, 'Marcus, I'm really sorry.

For doubting you, I mean.'

'Don't worry about it,' said Marcus, smiling. 'I mean, giants attacking London . . . it does sound quite far-fetched!'

'Still,' said Colin. 'Must have made you furious, no one believing you.'

There was a pause. Marcus grinned. 'Not as furious as Mum's going to be when she finds out about this.'

Colin shook his head. 'Doesn't bear thinking about,' he said. 'I wonder what she's doing now.'

'Minnie,' Marcus's mum whispered, shaking her gently. 'Minnie, wake up.'

Minnie pushed herself up in bed and rubbed her eyes.

'Sorry, sweetie, but we need to go on a little drive,' said Marcus's mum, helping Minnie out of bed. She passed her some clothes. 'Put these on over your PJs.'

Minnie pulled the coat on, blinking up with wide eyes. 'Are we going to see the giants?' she whispered.

Marcus's mum sighed. 'Something like that.'

CHAPTER TWENTY-EIGHT

'This is a nightmare,' Colin said as they circled above Westminster Bridge. 'There's nowhere to land.'

Marcus peered down, confirming every road was busy with traffic. The London Eye glittered among high-rise office blocks to their right. And to their left, Big Ben stood sentry beside the Houses of Parliament.

'There!' Marcus called out. 'The giants!'

Colin followed his gaze to the tall, dark shapes moving between the buildings south of the river. Incredibly – maybe because it was the middle of the night, and maybe because there was a storm brewing, so most people were home – the giants had apparently got this far without raising too much attention.

But as Tull emerged from behind a large circular office block on to the road leading to Westminster Bridge, surrounded by his band of giants, all that changed. Suddenly the giants were in plain view!

Cars honked their horns; cyclists pedalled frantically; Londoners out for a late-night stroll threw up their arms, screamed and ran!

Up ahead, traffic began to clear on the bridge as cars and taxis halted, reversed, and screeched back across the river!

'We need to land somewhere safe,' Marcus said, his voice tense.

Colin looked around frantically. 'I don't see anything! Wait, what about that park?' He pointed to a small patch of green space near the riverbank.

'It's too small, and there are people there,' Marcus replied, scanning for other options.

'Hold on tight!' Colin called out. 'I'm going in!'

'What?' said Marcus. 'Going in where?'

'The bridge!' exclaimed Colin. 'Look, it's empty!'

'Because the giants are about to cross it!'

'Unless you've got a better idea?' countered Colin.

Marcus felt his stomach turn. The bridge looked impossibly small, like something from a Lego set. He glanced back at Colin, but his stepfather-to-be seemed to be really enjoying himself, banking

235

right past the London Eye, then looping round to approach the bridge, the Thames glistening silver in the moonlight.

'Have you ever done anything like this before?' asked Marcus nervously, his whole body tensing as they skimmed the tops of the buildings, the crowd of giants below them heading directly to the bridge.

'Of course not!' exclaimed Colin. 'Are you insane? Who in their right mind would try and land on a road bridge in the middle of the Thames? It's raving lunacy!'

And with a wild laugh, he worked the joystick. Buildings and trees whipped past at an alarming rate. Marcus gripped the sides of his seat.

'One of the problems with Tiger Moths,' said Colin calmly as they dropped lower and lower, the crowd of giants rushing up towards them, the waves now visible on the surface of the river, 'is because they don't have any brakes, you have to land into the wind.'

'No brakes?!' yelped Marcus, his knuckles turning white.

'Hold tight – here we go!'

There was a shout from Marcus as they skimmed the giants' heads – then a loud bang as the undercarriage hit the tarmac, the plane bouncing back into the air, before landing for a second, third and fourth time in rapid succession, a lump forming in Marcus's throat as he fought the urge to be sick.

'Wow!' roared Colin, veering right and left as the wind brought the plane to a standstill. 'What a buzz!'

'Quick!' said Marcus, swiftly disconnecting his flight harness and climbing down on to the tarmac.

A sound like the beat of a distant drum filled the air.

Thump! Thump! Thump! Thump!

At the far end of the bridge, Tull and his gang of twenty-four giants had paused for a moment, their eyes fixed on their target. Then, with a sudden surge of motion, they had begun to advance once again, three and four abreast.

'Where are those friends of yours?' asked Colin, looking around nervously.

'I don't know,' said Marcus, hanging up his phone. 'No answer from Tilly!'

Thump! Thump! Thump! Thump!

The sound grew louder, the bridge vibrating as the army of giants drew closer.

Marcus rubbed his face in despair. 'What do we do?'

The giants were nearing the middle of the bridge.

Suddenly from somewhere behind them, there

was the screech of tyres and the *BEEPBEEPBEEP* of a car horn.

Marcus spun round to see a beautiful sight: a bright purple Volkswagen Beetle swerving to a halt beside them, his two friends leaning out of the windows and waving! The doors flew open, and out leaped Tilly, Rex and Mr Sheen, the three of them rushing forward and pressing the cape, staff and megaphone into Marcus's arms.

Colin removed his helmet, and came shyly up. 'Hello!' he said. 'I'm Colin.'

Marcus made awkward introductions as they all shook hands like they were at a tea party.

THUMP! THUMP!

As one, they turned.

THUMP! THUMP!

Tull was almost upon them!

'Sweet Merlin,' muttered Mr Sheen.

'Stay back here, all of you,' said Marcus, pulling on the cloak, and brandishing the staff and megaphone. 'Hide behind the plane.'

'Good luck, Marcus,' said Colin, giving his arm a squeeze. 'We'll be right here if you need us.'

'Good luck!' said Tilly and Rex, hugging him.

And Mr Sheen nodded and said, 'May Merlin be with you.'

Then they raced to safety, peeking out from behind the plane to take in the terrifying sight of Tull, flanked by twenty-three sky-high giants, stepping rapidly towards them.

THUMP! THUMP! THUMP! THUMP!

Marcus's body flushed with fear, and he fought the almost irresistible urge to run and hide behind the plane too.

Everything, and everyone, was depending on him.

Marcus took a deep breath, mustering every ounce of willpower and fighting every instinct in his body, and walked towards the crowd of giants, who shuffled to a halt in the middle of the bridge. Tull was right at the front, towering over him, but there was no sign of Crom.

There was a worried murmur from the giants as they took him in.

His cloak billowing around him, staff in hand, Marcus raised the megaphone to his lips.

'Hail, giants,' he bellowed. 'I am Mer—'

And then he paused. He tapped the megaphone. His voice was whipping away on the wind, just as it had done on top of the mound. The megaphone wasn't working!

'Ugh, this stupid thing,' muttered Marcus, propping the staff under his arm and bashing the megaphone with the palm of his hand.

'You have to press the little button!' called Mr Sheen, from behind the biplane.

Marcus frowned.

'On the handle!' explained Mr Sheen.

'Ah,' said Marcus, spotting it at last. 'Right, yes, thank you . . .'

This time pressing the little button, he spoke again, his voice now booming out into the night:

'HAIL, GIANTS. I AM MERLIN. LISTEN TO ME NOW OR I WILL IMPRISON YOU ONCE MORE . . . AND FOR ALL ETERNITY!'

CHAPTER TWENTY-NINE

For a second after Marcus had spoken, there was complete silence.

Then one of the giants emitted an ear-piercing scream and ran off, and the others too began slowly backing away.

'Have mercy, Mage!' whimpered one. 'Spare us, O Great One!' pleaded another.

'Call yourselves giants?' hissed Tull over his shoulder. 'Stand your ground!'

Tull frowned as he turned back towards the wizard.

'Merlin!' he called, warily. 'We meet again!'

Cowering in fear, the giants behind Tull began to retreat again the second his back was turned.

Feeling a surge of confidence, Marcus raised the megaphone and, looking directly at Tull, shouted, 'TURN BACK! TURN BACK, OR I SHALL BE FORCED TO CAST A SPELL ON YOU!'

Tull's resolve began to weaken . . . 'Okay, retreat, retreat,' he hissed over his shoulder, 'but slowly, and don't take your eyes off him.'

'It's working!' hissed Tilly as the giants began slowly backing up. 'It's really working!'

'THAT'S IT!' shouted Marcus, warming to his role. 'BE GONE, VILE OVERSIZED CREATURES!'

The giants were retreating more quickly now, and a couple at the back had turned and run.

But as Marcus raised the megaphone to speak again, a gust of wind blasted past him.

Tull's enormous nostrils twitched.

His eyes narrowing, the King of the Giants stopped. He took a step forward, and sniffed the air again. The other giants were sniffing now too. At last, Marcus managed to spot Crom among them. He was just behind Tull, and he was eyeing Marcus with a look of extreme concern.

'I SAID, GO BACK NOW!' Marcus commanded, but with less confidence. 'OR . . . OR . . . I WILL TURN YOU ALL INTO . . . INTO MICE!'

An evil smile played on Tull's lips. Crom, on the other hand, was now staring openly at Marcus, wide-eyed, shaking his head.

'OOOO don't hurt me, great wizard!' said Tull sarcastically.

Marcus gulped as Tull's shadow crept along the bridge towards him, the evil giant advancing step by step . . .

'I MEAN IT!' warbled Marcus, lifting the staff. 'I REALLY, REALLY MEAN IT . . .'

'Use your noses!' Tull called to the giants behind him. 'That isn't Merlin,' he shouted. 'It's Crom's friend – it's that boy!'

Tull's shadow was over him now, the giant's colossal frame blocking out the moon!

'I'M NOT!' trembled Marcus. 'I'M MERLIN! AND THAT'S IT! I'M PUTTING A SPELL ON YOU!'

He was now at Tull's feet, staring up helplessly.

'Fine, don't say I didn't warn you!' squeaked Marcus.

'Marcus, RUN!' shouted Colin.

The game was up. Marcus bolted, his staff and megaphone clattering to the ground as Tull's enormous hand lunged towards him!

But it was too late. Tull had seized him by the cape and was hoisting him high into the air!

Soon Marcus was kicking and struggling, the bridge swinging far below him, as he was brought face to face with the King of the Giants!

Tull smiled, his black teeth glinting between his thin green lips.

Marcus paled, his heart pounding so fast he thought it might burst from his chest.

'There's a little rhyme I like to say in these situations,' whispered Tull, savouring the moment. 'It's not the most sophisticated poem in the world, but it has a certain something.'

As the giant spoke, he dangled the boy above him, like a Roman emperor with a bunch of grapes.

'It goes like this,' Tull continued. '*Fee, Fi, Fo, Fum. I smell the blood of an Englishman!*'

Colin, Tilly, Rex and Mr Sheen all rushed to the giant's feet, beating his toes with their fists.

'Let him go, you brute!' shouted Tilly.

'As you wish.' Tull chuckled, tipping back his head. He closed his eyes in anticipation of his tasty snack and dropped Marcus into his gaping mouth.

'Help!' Marcus yelled as he plunged towards Tull's slimy, evil-smelling throat.

A moment later, Tull closed his mouth and swallowed. But there was nothing in it!

Tull opened his eyes. Crom was standing next to him, holding Marcus in the palm of his hand. Crom had snatched Marcus from the air as he fell, right under Tull's nose!

Marcus struggled to catch his breath, his chest heaving.

Crom placed his friend gently on the ground, and Colin and the others rushed forward to lead Marcus quickly away.

Then Crom turned back to Tull.

Tull growled menacingly as he closed the distance between them. He raised himself up to his full, terrifying height, and the two giants stood face to face, nose to nose, eye to eye.

The skies opened and it began to rain, heavy drops bouncing off the black tarmac.

CHAPTER THIRTY

Tull struck first. He lunged forward, pushing Crom so hard in the chest, he flew back into the crowd of giants. 'Traitor!' he barked.

As one, the band of giants pushed Crom forward to face Tull once more.

Marcus was slowly coming to now. He felt terrible. Crom had saved him. But at what cost? He saw fear flash in his friend's eyes.

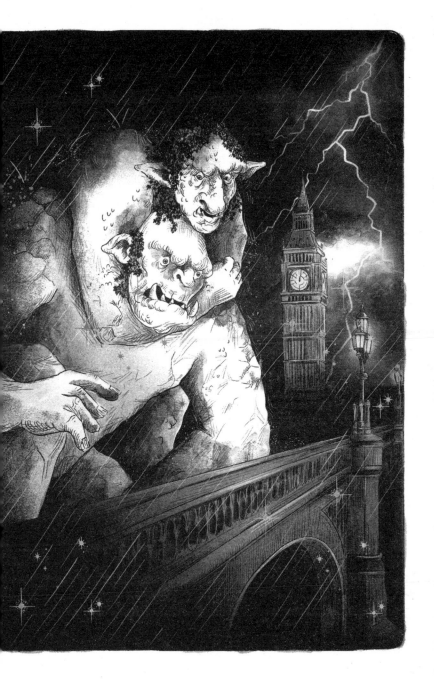

Crom slipped his arm around his opponent's neck

'Come on, Crom!' he roared. 'You can do this!'

Tull went to strike again, but Crom was ready for him this time. He stepped backwards, and Tull stumbled forward. As he did, Crom slipped his arm around his opponent's neck, gripping him in a headlock.

'Yes!' shouted Marcus from the sidelines. 'Go, Crom!'

Rex and Tilly were jumping up and down next to Marcus, shouting just as loudly, and Mr Sheen was telling Colin, 'That giant lives at my school, you know?'

Crom tightened his grip, and Tull's eyes began to bulge, his entire body shaking for air.

'Give in!' yelled Marcus. 'He's got you – give in!'

But Tull had no such intention. He jabbed his elbow hard into Crom's stomach. Crom recoiled in pain and released his grip.

It looked like the tide had turned. Shifting his weight, Tull shoved Crom again, winding him, then swiped his feet from under him, sending him smashing to the ground.

'Crom!!!' howled Marcus helplessly as Crom's colossal frame crashed down on to the tarmac.

Tull leered, kicking at Crom's motionless feet.

'Get up!' he crowed. 'Get up and fight!'

Behind Tull, the band of giants shouted and jeered, watching the fight with glee.

Crom groaned, waking up from his knockout. He rolled over on to his back, chest heaving.

'Get up!' roared Tull again.

Crom raised his head, his eyes clouded, his expression confused.

Slowly, deliberately, Tull stepped forward, placing his foot on Crom's windpipe.

'Leave him alone, you big bully!' shouted

Marcus, eyes blazing.

Eyes closed, fighting for air, Crom gripped Tull's leg, half attacking, half pleading.

But Tull pushed down, harder and harder, Crom flailing helplessly.

A giant-sized fury was building inside Marcus. He could not let this happen to his friend. Racking his brains for what to do, his eyes settled on the staff. At one end it was splintered and jagged from where he had smashed it against the school flagpole. Running to pick it up from where he'd dropped it earlier, he raced forward, driving the sharp end hard into Tull's foot!

'OWWWWWWWW,' squealed Tull, releasing Crom, and hopping around on one leg.

Crom leaped to his feet and, catching Tull off balance, pushed him hard in the chest.

Tull's eyes widened in horror as he felt himself

stagger backwards. Windmilling his arms wildly, he teetered on the edge of the bridge a moment before toppling backwards with an enormous splash into the swollen water of the River Thames.

'HELP! TULL CAN'T SWIM! SAVE TULL, PLEASE!'

The band of giants rushed to the edge of the bridge to watch their king thrashing in the water.

'Only if Tull admits defeat!' bellowed Crom.

'Please,' bawled Tull, reaching out as he thrashed and splashed, 'a hand, or Tull will drown!'

'Submit first,' repeated Crom.

'I submit!' hollered Tull, his eyes wide with panic. 'I submit.'

Crom smiled, savouring the moment. Stepping down from the bridge, he waded into the river and pulled Tull to his feet. The water was only thigh-deep!

As the water drained from his face, Tull's jaw fell open in surprise.

Unable to help themselves, the band of giants began to laugh.

'Silence!' commanded Crom, graciously helping Tull clamber back on to the bridge.

'You did it!' shouted Marcus, running over to his friend, who grinned broadly. 'You beat him!'

'All hail King Crom!' shouted one of the giants.

'Now, let's go destroy the humans!' shouted another.

'Yeah!' screamed the rest, cheering raucously.

Marcus shot Crom a meaningful look, Crom nodding in return, as if they shared an understanding.

'Wait,' said Crom, holding up a hand for silence. 'Crom is king now.'

The other giants murmured their agreement,

nodding in deference to their new ruler.

Crom reached down and lifted Marcus up, placing him gently on his shoulder.

Marcus felt a surge of pride and loyalty towards his friend.

Crom raised his hand, and the giants fell silent.

'Listen to Boy,' he commanded. 'He has something to say.'

CHAPTER THIRTY-ONE

As if the weather itself was eager to hear what Marcus had to say, the rain immediately stopped, the wind ceased, and a bright moon emerged from behind the clouds.

Marcus was one of those boys with an answer for everything, but now, in the silvery moonlight, with the eye of every giant upon him, he suddenly found himself lost for words. What could he possibly say that could change their minds?

Then he caught sight of Mr Sheen, edging out from behind the plane, flanked by Colin, Tilly and Rex, and suddenly he knew.

'Look,' he said. 'Let's talk.'

The giants grunted, but Marcus continued.

'What Merlin did was wrong. And I'm sorry.'

One or two of the giants looked at one another, puzzled. No one had ever spoken to them like this before.

'What's really going on here?' said Marcus. 'Behind all the acting out, I mean.'

There was a long silence. Marcus sighed.

'You need to talk about it, or this anger is going to eat you up!'

There were some murmurs from up at the back, and then one of the giants shouted, 'Someone cut down all my trees!'

And another: 'I don't like all the bright lights!'

And still another: 'Those whizzy things are so loud!'

'Cars?' said Crom helpfully.

'Yeah, cars!'

'Okay, okay,' said Marcus, raising his arms, asking for a chance to speak.

'Change can be scary. But you can't turn back the clock. Life moves on, things change, people change. But maybe, if you give things a chance, open yourself up to new experiences, you might discover that it's not as bad as you think? You might even enjoy it . . . ?'

There was a deafening silence.

'No way!' called a giant. 'Too bright and noisy!'

'Kill the humans!' added another.

'Crom is king!' boomed a third. 'So Crom decides!'

There was a pause as all eyes turned to Crom.

For a few moments the giant bowed his head, deep in thought. Then, raising his eyes, he said:

'Crom thinks we should be a pally dimmo . . . What did you call it?'

'A parliamentary democracy?' offered Marcus.

'Yes,' said Crom. 'Where giants talk, then decide.'

'Interestingly enough, the Houses of Parliament are actually right there,' said Colin, pointing in the direction of Big Ben.

The giants all said, 'Hmm,' and turned to look with mild interest, then turned back to Crom again.

Crom thought for a moment, turning Colin's suggestion over in his mind, then nodded. 'Okay,' he said. 'Giants will talk.'

'Yes, Galligantus,' said Crom, pointing to one of the band of giants who had raised their hands, each asking to speak.

The new King of the Giants was sitting on the grass beside the Houses of Parliament, surrounded by his subjects.

'Humans are idiots,' said the bald-headed giant Crom had pointed at. 'Who needs them?'

'The rate they're cutting down trees, they'll all be gone soon anyway,' added a heavy-set giant with a long, braided beard.

'Cowards!' declared Tull. 'There's only one way to do this: DESTROY ALL HUMANS!'

'Maybe . . .' said a top-knotted giant, thinking it over. 'Maybe giants should sleep for another thousand years and see what the world looks like then?'

'We'll probably have the place to ourselves!'

exclaimed a thin giant with high cheekbones and scraped-back hair.

'Very well, enough talking,' said Crom, silencing them with a gesture. 'Now giants vote. Hands up giants who want to destroy all humans . . .'

Tull's hand immediately rose, followed by a couple of others.

'Hands up giants who want to go back to their mounds and sleep until humans destroy themselves.'

A forest of hands appeared.

'Then it's decided,' said Crom. 'Giants go back to sleep.'

A few mutterings rippled around the group.

'Phew, what a relief!'

'I know! I was tired before we left . . .'

Then, one by one, the giants heaved themselves to their feet and began the slow march back across the bridge, heading for their various homes.

A big cheer went up, and Marcus turned to see Colin, Mr Sheen, Rex and Tilly running towards him.

'You did it!' squealed Tilly, giving him an enormous hug.

'Respect,' said Rex with a high-five.

'Very impressive.' Mr Sheen beamed, pumping him by the hand. Then, leaning in closer, he said under his breath, 'Consider your expulsion rescinded.'

'Fantastic!' replied Marcus, adding in a whisper, 'What does that mean?'

'It means there's a permanent place for you at Merlin's,' said Mr Sheen. 'If you want it.'

Marcus was just about to play it cool and tell Mr Sheen he'd let him know when he heard a polite cough high above him, rumbling like thunder. He turned to see Crom, his enormous face creased in a delighted smile, and knew immediately that his friend had come to say goodbye.

CHAPTER THIRTY-TWO

'Greetings, King Crom,' said Marcus, sweeping his arm extravagantly and bowing at the waist.

Crom grinned.

'Thanks for saving my life again,' added Marcus.

'Thanks for saving Crom's – and talking to giants. Now giants can go back to sleep. Sleep is better than fighting . . . Fighting is very tiring.'

Crom tried to stifle a yawn.

'You should go,' said Marcus sadly. 'Get some sleep.'

Crom nodded. 'Boy won't be around when Crom wakes up again,' he said sadly.

'I guess not,' said Marcus, kicking at the ground.

'Well goodbye, Boy.'

'Goodbye, King Crom.'

Crom took a deep breath, looking out across the city.

'Crom will miss the lights,' he said. 'The lights are pretty.'

Then Crom turned and began walking back towards the bridge.

'Er, excuse me . . . Mr Crom?'

Crom turned.

'Sorry, you don't know me,' said Mr Sheen. 'I run the school where your mound is . . .'

'Hi, yes, nice to meet you . . .'

267

Ben Miller

'Um, I don't suppose, if you're going our way . . . ? Could we possibly . . . ?'

'No problem,' said Crom, smiling.

'Marvellous!' called Mr Sheen, hurrying towards the car and motioning for Rex and Tilly to join. 'See you back at Merlin's, Marcus!'

'See you at Merlin's!' shouted Rex and Tilly, waving through the window of the car as Crom picked it up in his enormous hand, tucked it carefully under his arm, and ambled back across the bridge, heading for home.

Marcus watched in silence until his friends had disappeared from sight.

Colin put a hand on his shoulder, and this time Marcus didn't shrug it off. Colin smiled.

'Come on then,' he said gently. 'I'd better get you home.'

Which was when they heard shouting

coming from behind them.

'Marcus! Colin!'

They spun round. Marcus's mum and Minnie were running towards them.

'Are you okay?' his mum asked, rushing towards Marcus and hugging him tight. 'I couldn't sleep for worrying, so we decided to drive down here too . . . but there was a roadblock, and we couldn't get through. We had to leave the car and walk! We heard there was some sort of . . .'

She looked up and down the bridge, trying to make sense of it all.

'I mean, there weren't *actually* any . . . ? Is everything okay?'

'Where are the giants?' asked Minnie, looking around.

'Sorry,' said Colin, dropping a kiss on her forehead, 'you just missed them.'

'Not FAIR!' said Minnie.

Then to Marcus's mum Colin added, 'You would NOT believe the night we've had.'

She raised an eyebrow.

'I'll tell you later,' he said.

But Marcus's mum had caught sight of the yellow Tiger Moth sitting proudly on the bridge. 'What on earth is a plane doing . . . ?' She trailed off as she looked at it more closely, her eyes widening. 'Colin, that's not . . . ?'

Colin cleared his throat. 'I've got something to tell you, Abigail,' he said.

'He flies planes!' said Minnie, unable to keep the secret.

Marcus's mum frowned. 'But . . .' she began.

'I should have told you,' said Colin. 'I'm sorry.'

'You lied to me,' said his mum, the colour draining from her face. 'The one thing I asked of you—'

'But, Mum,' said Marcus, cutting her off. 'It wasn't a bad lie. It was a good one. He just didn't want to worry you.'

She frowned. 'Is that true?'

Colin nodded sheepishly. 'Like I say, I'm sorry.'

Marcus's mum blinked. She looked between her son and her fiancé and back again. Colin lowered his eyes. Marcus smiled hopefully.

'Well,' she said. 'I suppose you'd better fly us all home then.'

They were about to leave, when a van screeched up, a reporter leaping out of the back, flanked by a cameraman and a sound technician, the light on the camera dazzling Marcus's eyes.

'Clive Bacon!' he yelled. 'Channel Twelve News. Have you seen anything . . . unusual?'

'Like what?' asked Marcus innocently.

The reporter looked awkward. 'Oh, I don't

know . . . just . . . anything unusual?'

Marcus thought carefully. Much as Crom loved lights, he might not appreciate this sort of attention.

'No,' he said, shaking his head.

'No,' echoed Colin, his mum and Minnie, shaking their heads too.

'Thought not,' said the reporter, glancing around at the empty bridge and deserted streets. 'Giants,' he said to his workmates, giving a little laugh and shaking his head in amusement. 'I told you: there's no such thing.'

EPILOGUE

'You may now kiss the bride,' said Mr Sheen through his megaphone, his red-and-crimson cloak blowing in the wind as he anointed the happy couple with his newly-mended staff.

Colin lifted Marcus's mum's veil, and planted a juicy kiss right on her lips.

There was a burst of applause, led by the Teatime Assortment, as the large crowd of friends, family and schoolchildren gathered on the top of Merlin's Mound all showed their appreciation.

As if by magic, a gust of wind threw handfuls of hawthorn blossom as if it were confetti, swirling and dancing in the air.

Marcus grinned up at Minnie, who had an excellent view of proceedings from her spot on his shoulders.

'And now,' said Mr Sheen, 'it's time for some music from . . . the Notables!'

'Come on, Marcus,' said Tilly into the microphone. 'Come and join us onstage! You know you want to!'

Marcus shook his head.

'Still no. I mean – respect. But no. Always going to be no. For ever no.'

There were chuckles from the audience.

'Suit yourself,' said Tilly with a smile. 'One,

two, three, four . . .' she called, and the band crashed into their first number. Everyone winced for a moment as it was rather louder and thrashier than they were expecting, but they soon got used to it, Colin spinning Marcus's mum round and round, Minnie squealing as Marcus bounced her up and down on his shoulders. Even Marcus's dad had a bit of a dance after he realized that literally no one wanted to talk about fridge-freezers.

As Marcus swayed to the beat, the music ringing out around him, surrounded by his friends and family, he noticed that the mound seemed to be shaking, and he couldn't help but wonder if maybe the shaking wasn't *just* because of all the people dancing . . .

Marcus bent down and put a hand to the earth. He smiled a knowing smile and, closing his eyes for just a moment, let his mind drift down to where his old friend was sleeping peacefully, dreaming of songbirds, babbling brooks and pristine forests, his foot tapping away in time to the music.

ACKNOWLEDGEMENTS

The beginnings of this story are to be found in the pages of *King Arthur* by Roger Lancelyn Green, which my father read to me each night when I was around ten years old. The tales of King Arthur and his Knights of the Round Table and their relentless quests for glory seemed at the same time utterly fantastical and absolutely true, and the fact that their author sounded like he might be a knight himself only added to my sense of wonder. Thank you, Sir Roger, and thank you, Dad.

That said, the adventure on these pages really started to take shape when I stumbled across the Marlborough Mound, a Stone Age monument stranded amongst the striking red brick buildings of Marlborough College, in Wiltshire. When I heard there was another, almost identical mound in Silbury, just a few miles away, and that another hill in nearby Wilcot was called the Giant's Grave, I began to wonder what might really be under all that innocent-looking green turf ...

My Lady of the Lake, holding the Excalibur of writing-time-in-the-shed above the broiling waters of family life – and her own full-on career – is my wife Jess; my gratitude as ever, for all her patient encouragement, wise counsel, and good humour. Thank you also to my children – Jackson, Harrison, and Lana – who listened to lots of early drafts and didn't hold back with their praise, or more to the point, their criticism. There's nothing like having your own son or daughter wander off while you're reading a passage you've slaved over to focus the mind.

Swearing allegiance to the publishing Camelot that is Simon & Schuster Children's has been the making of me as an author. We are indeed a Round Table, united in our collective endeavour, although Rachel Denwood is definitely in charge. I bend low, sweeping the plume of my helmet before my steadfast editorial knights, Lucy Pearse and Lily Morgan, supported valiantly by Arub Ahmed, Michelle Misra, Kathy Webb, Veronica Lyons, and Olive Childs. My favour also do I give to Ali Dougal and to the exemplary S&S Children's design department, with extra acknowledgments to Sorrel Packham.

Sarah Macmillan, Dan Fricker, and Emma Finnerty: your strategic prowess in marketing is lauded. Eve Wersocki Morris, my humble thanks for taming the PR dragon. To the sales heroes, Laura Hough, Dani Wilson, Leanne Nulty, Richard Hawton, Nicholas Hayne, and Caitlin Withey —

my deepest thanks. This book ushers in what I fervently hope will be an exciting era of collaboration with Elisa Paganelli, whose enchanting illustrations have given the story a whole new dimension. Thank you, Elisa, for joining our merry band; I eagerly anticipate our future projects.

Every Arthur needs his Merlin, and I've found mine in the form of the sage Luigi Bonomi and his enthusiastic team at LBA books. Thanks also to Clementine Ahearne and Alice Natali at the Intercontinental Literary Agency who have carried this and many other of my tales to readers in distant lands. I remain in the debt of that indomitable trio Samira Davies, Alice Burton, and Geri Spicer at Independent Talent Group. Heartfelt thanks also to my ever-inventive heralds Amanda Squires and Clair Dobbs at CLD Communications; Rosie Robinson, my social media minstrel; and Tasha Brade, my trusty squire-ess.

Lastly, a mighty hurrah to you, my noble readers. As the seasons turn, I look forward to meeting many more of you at tournaments, feasts, and places of learning worldwide. May we join in many more adventures together! Your passion for reading, your sense of justice, and your curiosity about the world spur me onward. One day, mark my words, you will be giants.

CHRISTMAS DELIVERED
WITH FESTIVE BESTSELLERS FROM
BEN MILLER

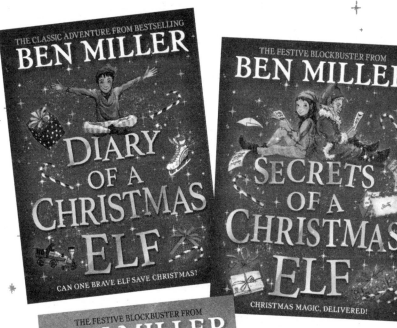

OUT OCTOBER 2023